Marrying Raven

Brides of Clearwater Book 2

Melanie D. Snitker

Marrying Raven
(Brides of Clearwater Book 2)
© 2018 Melanie D. Snitker

Published by
Dallionz Media, LLC
P.O. Box 6821
Abilene, TX 79608

Blue Valley Author Services
www.bluevalleyauthorservices.com/

Melanie D. Snitker
melaniedsnitker@gmail.com
www.melaniedsnitker.com

ISBN-13: 978-0-9975289-9-2

This book is dedicated to all
who embrace second chances.

Chapter One

Raven Weber leaned against the counter and checked the messages on her phone while she waited for her order. Clearwater Coffee, one of the most popular coffee shops in town, bustled with activity around her. The cappuccino machine whirred, a microwave dinged, and all the while, sounds of patrons visiting filled the air.

Someone called her name, and she waved in response. This was the kind of atmosphere she loved. Having grown up in Clearwater, she was bound to run into someone she knew just about everywhere she went. Especially in this neighborhood merely blocks from her parents' house.

Raven wished she could relax for a while, but she needed to get back to work. She stood on her toes to see past the machines on the other side of the counter. Chrissy, one of Raven's close friends, secured the lid on the last of four cups of coffee and placed it in the carrier before approaching the counter. Her black hair, complete with purple, pink, and blue streaks, shone under the lights above.

"Here you go. This one," Chrissy tapped one lid with a brightly-colored fingernail, "is yours." She glanced over to make sure no one was waiting to order and then rested an elbow on the counter. "I don't know how you consume that much caffeine in one beverage."

"It's a gift." Raven grinned, resisting the urge to snatch the cup out of the carrier and take a swig of the hot drink right now. Everyone who knew Raven well also knew her penchant for coffee. She didn't start her day without it, and she needed a fix midway through the afternoon as well. Thankfully, the ladies she worked with didn't mind. They put their own orders in, and Raven happily did the fetching, especially if it meant getting out of the office for a few minutes.

The bell above the shop's door rang as a new customer entered. Chrissy noticed him perusing the menu before turning her attention back to Raven. "You and Wade going out tonight?"

Raven would normally be looking forward to a date with her boyfriend on a Friday night. She wrinkled her nose. "I don't think so. Maybe tomorrow."

Chrissy looked surprised. "Something going on between you two?"

Raven shrugged. It'd take more than a text-based conversation for her to know the answer to that. "He's been busy with work. We haven't talked much the last couple of weeks. I'm half expecting him to call and suggest a movie or something." Maybe. Probably not. She wasn't sure which was worse: that he wasn't calling, or that she wasn't sure she cared.

The customer who'd come in a minute ago stepped up to the counter. He made eye contact with Chrissy and gave her an entirely inappropriate smile. "Hey, baby. I'm ready to order."

Chrissy raised an eyebrow at Raven. "Looks like I need to sell someone some manners."

Raven covered a laugh with one hand. Her friend may be barely over five feet tall, but between the colorful hair, bright nails, rings on every finger, and attitude, she was more like a bouncer than a coffee barista. "You tell him, girl." Raven picked up the drink carrier and gave her friend a smile. "Thanks again."

"You're welcome. Don't work too hard."

Raven raised a hand in farewell as she turned to leave the coffee shop. Mrs. Meridian, Raven's biology teacher in high school, stopped her. Even though she was retired now, Mrs. Meridian remained active in community projects.

Raven's former teacher patted her hand. "Have you run into Heath yet? I heard he's getting out of the house now. I imagine that horrible surgery left him on his back for a while."

Raven resisted the urge to tell Mrs. Meridian that she hoped she wouldn't cross paths with Heath Shaw, but it was no use. The older woman was already speaking again.

"I ran into his daddy the other day. Heath is hoping to be back on the field as soon as he can. That boy was always determined."

Determined. That's not how Raven would word it. Just thinking about her ex-fiancé had her clenching her teeth. He should've stayed in Cleveland and recovered from his injury there instead of returning to Clearwater. He'd probably only come back to get the sympathy from his many adoring fans.

Not that she was bitter. The day he'd broken off their engagement and walked out of her life was one of the most painful days of her life. But over the twelve years since, she'd realized Heath had done her a favor. If he was that dedicated to playing football and leaving his hometown behind, it would've happened eventually. It's good he was in a hurry to leave again because it meant Raven might not have to run into him at all.

Mrs. Meridian seemed to wait for a response.

Raven forced a smile. "Yes, once Heath sets his mind to something, there's no stopping him."

Mrs. Meridian's smile widened as she patted Raven on the shoulder. "Well, you've got your hands full there, dear. I'll let you go. Don't work too hard now."

"I won't, Mrs. Meridian. You have a great day."

Maybe the coffee shop wasn't the best place to hang around if Heath was the talk of the town. She left and walked the block and a half to Clearwater Rehabilitation Center. While Clearwater may not be a huge city, supporting a population of just over 25,000 people, the CRC was one of the best centers in the Texas Hill Country. The office was consistently busy with patients seeking help in their process of healing from injury.

It was a great place to work, and it allowed her to do what she loved without leaving her hometown.

She'd started handing out coffee to her co-workers when their boss, Fay Bright, breezed into the room. "We've got a new patient today in room seven. Ruptured Achilles tendon. He's two weeks into recovery, so we'll take things slow at first." She traded the iPad mini for the cup of coffee Raven held out to her. "I evaluated his injury. Can you take care of the exercises for me?"

Raven accepted the iPad from Fay and glanced through the list of exercises. These would be simple enough, although it seemed like a lot for someone who had had surgery recently. Wait, Achilles tendon? Four weeks? Surely not. Even as she tried to convince herself she was being paranoid, her stomach tightened.

Fay must have thought she was reacting to the exercise regimen. "Nope, that's right. He's in a hurry to get his leg back to normal again. I've set up an intense therapy timeline. We'll stick with it unless we see any reason to do otherwise."

Raven would've objected, but Fay excused herself and went to her next patient. That left Raven standing there holding an iPad and trying to convince herself to scroll up and look at the patient's name.

Instead, she took her own cup of coffee, tossed the carrier into the trash, and headed for room seven. The world wouldn't possibly be this cruel to her. There were plenty of sports where an incident could rupture the Achilles tendon. CRC was the best rehabilitation center around, and it got patients from hundreds of miles away. This guy could be anyone.

Confident she was being silly, she scrolled up on the patient information as she opened the door, searching for the name before she could introduce herself. "Hello—" The air whooshed from her lungs as she looked from the words she could scarcely believe to the man himself.

Yep, it was Heath Shaw sitting in the chair. He was the boy she'd grown up with. The man she'd fallen in love with and promised to marry. He was also the man who'd walked away from her—from them. All over a *potential* football career.

Waves of resentment crashed into her. This was the heart of Texas, and her brother-in-law coached the local high school football team. That meant Raven attended way more football games than she cared to. But she'd purposefully avoided seeing a single NFL game over the last twelve years.

The last thing she needed was to watch Heath on TV. She hadn't wanted to see him then, and she sure didn't want to see him now. As far as she knew, this was the first time he'd bothered to step a toenail in Clearwater. Clearly, he hadn't been in a hurry to reunite with her, either. It could just as easily have been another dozen years if his injury hadn't mucked things up.

All right, God. I know You like to keep me hopping, but this? I'm seriously questioning Your sense of humor right now.

Unfortunately, Heath was still in the room. All this time should've aged the man. But there he sat, looking every bit as much of a handsome jock now as he had their senior year. His sandy brown hair needed a cut, the ends curling slightly over the top of his ears. And those blue eyes…

…were watching her every move.

Oh, good grief. How long had she been standing there staring at him? Well, if the bewildered expression on his face was any indication, he was as surprised to see her.

Her hurricane of emotions hovered over irritation as she focused on why he'd left their hometown. She took another leisurely drink of her coffee and wished she'd had Chrissy add a third shot of espresso. After placing the cup on the counter, along with the iPad, Raven crossed her arms and studied her patient. "Heath."

"Raven." He cleared his throat and shifted his booted foot on the floor. "I had no idea you worked here. I didn't even know you'd become a PT." He cleared his throat again.

He hadn't kept up with what she was doing. Nice to know his plan to cut her out of his life had been so complete. She raised an eyebrow. "Technically, I'm a physical therapist assistant. I've been working here for the last four years."

"If I'd known…" His sentence trailed off.

If he'd known, he would've what? Gone somewhere else for therapy? Asked for a different PTA? Stayed out of Clearwater completely? Raven swallowed a retort. He was here for therapy, and she was his assigned therapist. At least for today. *Be professional, Raven. The quicker you get the guy through therapy, the sooner he'll be out of your life. Again.* Besides, he was probably trying to recover enough to get back to Cleveland.

She picked up the iPad and propped one hip on the counter. "Your chart says you were injured during a football game, but no complications during surgery to repair your Achilles. We've got a rigid therapy schedule set up for you. Are you sure you're up to therapy twice a week?"

Heath sat up straighter, pride flashing in his eyes. "I'll come in as often as I can. I want to get rid of these crutches." A tendon in his neck twitched as he clenched his jaw. A sure sign her question had aggravated him.

Good.

"I'm sure you're ready to get back on the field as soon as possible." Okay, that edge to her voice might not have been entirely professional. Raven sighed and lowered the iPad. "Look, if you'd rather have a different PTA, I can speak with Fay this evening." She wasn't sure what kind of response she was looking for. If he agreed, it'd be another dismissal to add to the list.

But if he was fine with her managing his PT, then she'd have to deal with seeing him for the next few weeks.

His blue eyes blinked in surprise. "I want the person who can best help me recover my strength."

Fay insisted Raven was the best PT assistant she'd ever had working for her, and that's why she'd arranged it this way. Well, Raven would do her job. She'd help her patient the way she was trained and push past the fact that it's Heath. She could do that, right?

"Then we should get started." Raven withdrew some pamphlets from one of the cabinets. "These are for you to take home. I'm sure your doctor has gone over the kind of recovery you can expect from this type of injury."

"Yeah." Heath took the pamphlets from her, folded them, and slipped them into a back pocket.

She checked the iPad. "Looks like you'll be in every Tuesday and Thursday starting next week. I see that Dr. Bright adjusted your boot. Make sure you continue to sleep in it and let us know if you experience any pain at the incision site. Sometimes adjustments can cause the boot to rub it, and we can fix that easily enough."

"Will do."

"Let me know if you experience a lot of discomfort during the sessions, and we'll back off a little."

"I think I'll manage." Heath's displeasure showed through, and it deepened his voice. There were many times in school when he'd stood up for her, and his voice would deepen like that as he confronted her tormentors.

The memory sent an unexpected tendril of warmth through her, and she frowned. "I'm sure you will. You're good at that."

"At what?" There was no missing the challenge in his eyes or the way his large hands curled around the arm of his chair.

Raven realized it would take little to turn this to a discussion that was long overdue. A discussion she had no intention of ever having for fear of opening old wounds. She ignored his question. "All right, let's get started. We have a section of indoor track on the other side of the building. We'll work on putting some weight on that foot while you're walking and see how that goes. Then we'll go to the gym after that to start on upper body and upper extremity circuit training."

He reached for the crutches that were leaning against the wall nearby and used them to get to a standing position. "Let's do this."

Raven stifled a sigh. If she'd known this would be waiting for her today, she might've climbed back in bed this morning.

God, we're going to have ourselves a little chat later.

~*~

Heath couldn't stop stealing glimpses of the woman he hadn't seen in years. Raven seemed as self-assured as ever. Growing up, she'd been the one girl in school who didn't care what everyone else was doing. She knew what she wanted, and she was content to be herself. He'd hated that some of their classmates focused on those differences and teased her about them. Especially when they'd drawn Heath to her in the first place.

Now her ability to pretend something didn't bother her frustrated him. She'd been the last person he expected to see walk through that door. He knew he'd end up running into her eventually, but he'd banked on later. That's what he got for not keeping tabs on her. If he'd known she was a PT assistant here, he might've gone somewhere else for therapy. This whole thing had thrown him for a loop. Now he was second-guessing nearly every decision he'd made in the last twelve years. It was clear she wasn't happy to see him. Yet here she was, carrying on professionally as she explained everything to him and then helped him with his gait. All business.

He caught a whiff of lavender. It'd always been her favorite flower, and the scent had haunted him for months after he'd left.

Heath hoped he appeared every bit as stoic as she did. Seeing her had been a shock, and it dawned on him that he'd be working with her twice a week. Yeah, if anyone needed incentive to make a fast recovery, he had it.

He listened as Raven gave him directions, and he showed that he understood what to do. The track they were using ran the length of the hallway, and he'd walked it three or four times. Heath's leg and foot already ached. He wasn't about to admit it, though. He'd known therapy wouldn't be easy, but he hadn't expected it to be this difficult, either. He swallowed his aggravation.

When Raven announced they'd finished with that part of his therapy, Heath released a slow lungful of air. "Great. To the gym, then?"

"To the gym." Raven slipped the small iPad into a pocket of her colorful scrubs and then led the way.

Heath took stock of the equipment as they entered. Maybe it was nothing like the training gym he used in Cleveland with his teammates, but this was still a great setup. There were three other people using the equipment.

Raven waved to a man in scrubs who returned the gesture. "There are always people here who can help if you need it." She pointed to the piece of equipment that resembled an upright bicycle. "Start out with the upper body ergometer. That'll help you maintain your fitness level while we wait for that tendon to heal. You can do upper extremity circuit training afterward, but make sure you don't overdo it, especially this first week."

Her caution irked him. He knew his own limitations, thank you very much. "I think I'm set."

He took in the room as he avoided her dark brown eyes. She hadn't changed much. Her face was fuller, her hair shorter, but it all suited her nicely. He finally allowed his gaze to connect with hers. It was the hardness in her eyes that bothered him. She'd always been fun-loving. Outgoing. She thrived on making others laugh. He saw none of that now. Was it because of him and their unusual situation, or had her personality shifted like everything else?

The one change that snagged his attention the most, though, was the little scar near the right corner of her mouth. He used to have every contour of those lips memorized, and that hadn't been there before. What had caused the scar?

He glanced at her left hand. No wedding ring, not that it meant anything.

He pulled his thoughts back on track. She was probably being cool toward him because of their history. Honestly? He deserved that and a whole lot more.

Raven blinked several times, took a step back, and slipped her hands into her pockets. "I'll see you on Thursday then." With that, she turned and left the gym.

Heath watched her walk away, frustrated how, even after twelve years, that sway of hers still captured his attention.

Maybe Raven's suggestion of seeing a different assistant wasn't such a bad one after all. The rehabilitation center was busy, there had to be more PTs he could work with. It'd be a whole lot easier on him and Raven that way. Yes, as soon as he finished here, he'd make different arrangements. His decision bolstered his mood a little as he went to work.

He got through the ergometer and did some

circuit training as well, but it took Heath longer than he thought it should have. He made a mental note to bring a duffle bag with a change of clothes next time. Changing into a fresh shirt after exercising was a must. Once his foot was out of the boot, he'd take a shower before heading to his parents' house, too. He couldn't wait until something as normal as taking a shower was no longer the production it was now.

He headed to the front of the building and the check-in counter. Raven was nowhere to be seen. He smiled at the receptionist. "Hi, I'm starting physical therapy this week. I was wondering if it would be possible to be assigned to a different assistant."

The woman at the desk stared at him, her brows disappearing into the bangs that lay piled on her forehead. "I...I don't know if we do that." She glanced at the other receptionist who was busy with a phone call. "Give me a moment." She disappeared into the back. When she returned, she brought Dr. Bright with her.

The doctor seemed concerned. "Is there something I can help you with, Mr. Shaw?"

"I was asking about being assigned to a different assistant for my future appointments."

"Did Raven fail to give you proper help or instructions?"

Heath may not want to work with Raven for a variety of reasons, but she seemed more than capable of doing her job. "No, of course not. There's some history with our families, and I thought it might be easier if we changed things up." That sounded lame even to his own ears.

Dr. Bright shook her head. "I'm sorry, but setting everything up for you on short notice took some work with the schedule. I may be able to swap things around, but it could delay the start of your therapy."

The other receptionist had finished her phone call and was watching them. Nothing like having an audience. Heath wished he'd never asked in the first place. He should've gone home and called in with his question. "No, I don't want a delay." The waiting room suddenly seemed stuffy, and he glanced toward the exit. "I thought I'd ask. Thank you both. Have a great day."

He turned and, crutches under his arms, got out of there as fast as his booted foot would carry him.

As he waited outside for his ride back to the house, Raven's lovely face came to mind. Brown eyes the color of dark chocolate looked back at him. The combination of those beautiful orbs and the dark hair that framed her face... His chest ached with the memories he struggled to keep at bay.

Before he'd come back to Clearwater, it'd taken everything in him to not research and confirm she still lived in town. Heath wasn't surprised she did though. She'd always loved this place. Sworn she'd raise her family here. There was no reason for him to think she'd have done otherwise. In fact, even without the wedding ring on her finger, she was likely happily married with a baby waiting for her at home. He imagined her carefree spirit pulling those full lips of hers into a smile.

He shoved thoughts of how often he'd kissed those very lips into the dusty closet of his brain where they belonged. The past was the past, and it would be a lot easier on Heath if he'd accept that, work through physical therapy, and get out of Clearwater again as soon as possible.

Chapter Two

Heath pulled open the front door to Shaw Camping and Outdoor. Familiar scents immediately greeted him as an old friend might have. He inhaled deeply, relishing the smell of leather, canvas, and gun oil.

He'd come home two weeks ago to recover from surgery. Without a home of his own in town, and temporarily unable to drive, he grudgingly moved into his parents' house. The couch he was sleeping on in the office made his back ache. Staying at the house he grew up in was strangely awkward. But this right here? Entering the store he'd spent much of his childhood in was the very definition of coming home.

Memories of hours spent as a young child helping his father, Gabe Shaw, hang tackle on the displays or greeting customers came to mind. It was those memories he'd clung to while he was away, back when his father was content to let Heath be a kid. They'd been close then as they'd planned the adventures they wanted to go on someday. It seemed like a lifetime ago. Yet little had changed in the store. It was as if Heath had stepped into a photograph. He shook his head in amazement.

His trip down memory lane ended abruptly when his father's voice brought Heath's attention to the customer service counter. "You going to let in all that hot air, son?"

Heath put his weight on the crutches and managed to hobble through the door. It'd been almost four weeks since his surgery, and Heath still felt awkward walking with the blasted things. Of course, the boot encasing his left foot certainly didn't help matters any. He was used to spending hours in the gym, running across the field, and going through drills with his teammates. The inability to walk through a door with any amount of grace was infuriating.

His father shook Mr. Crosby's hand and wished him well. A longtime customer, old Mr. Crosby stopped to greet Heath. "It's good to see you. Been too long since we've had our star running back in Clearwater." He chuckled and gave Heath a hearty pat on the back. "I'd say I hoped you'd stick around, but I guess you've got more important things to do. You get to feeling better, you hear?"

"Yes, sir."

Mr. Crosby waved again to Pop and called over his shoulder, "Have a good Thursday, Gabe."

Heath smiled and watched as the man left the air-conditioned store for the warm September air. He might have wondered what Mr. Crosby meant by better things to do, except the older gentleman had teased Heath for as long as he could remember.

Heath had been popular enough when he played football in their little town back in high school. After that, he'd gotten a full ride to Portland State University. There he worked toward a business degree while playing college football. The day he got drafted into the NFL, Heath thought his dreams had come true. But playing as a backup and bouncing from team to team wasn't what he'd expected.

The latest team to pick him up in Cleveland meant real play time on the field. Finally, he was doing what he'd been working toward all his life. That's when he ruptured his Achilles tendon.

Sometimes life punched you right in the gut.

He'd had no idea how much this town had made him out to be a hero. The attention he'd received since his return was way more than he cared for. Pop said there was a restaurant or two around town with Heath's photo and name up on the wall. Heath wished he knew which restaurants they were, so he could avoid them.

When Heath turned back to his father, the frown greeting him morphed his own smile into one that matched.

"You shouldn't be here." There was no missing the disapproval on his father's face. "You should go home and rest up after your appointment. The sooner you get into shape, the sooner you'll be back on the field." He fixed Heath with a look that demanded respect. "I expect you to put all your efforts into recovery."

Heath fought against the waves of annoyance and sadness as they crashed into each other. He'd hoped his father might have mellowed after twelve years. Apparently that'd been nothing but a pipe dream. His father may not have changed, but Heath wasn't that little boy whose happiness was built around his father's approval. He'd learned long ago that goal would always hover out of reach.

Heath had every intention of doing what he could to recover as fast as possible. "I'm fine, Pop." He'd been lying around his parents' house since the surgery and didn't look forward to going back. As much as he enjoyed catching up with Mom, he couldn't handle being around Pop every evening.

He'd started looking for a place of his own—he could certainly afford it. Besides, it'd be worth the peace even if he only lived there for the next month or two and then held onto it in case he came back for a visit. "I know these physical therapists will want me up and moving. I figured I'd stop by the store and see how it looks." Heath's gaze roamed the large space, taking in the bright overhead lights and the aisles of camping, hunting, and fishing equipment. While everything was clean and orderly, Heath noticed that the shelving could use a new coat of paint. In fact, the flooring was looking worn as well.

His father had always taken great pride in the

store. Heath was surprised to see it look this worn down. Was Pop having financial trouble? The thought bothered him, but there was no way he could ask without seriously wounding his father's pride.

After playing for the NFL, Heath was not hurting for money. He'd taken financial advice and invested in several properties around Clearwater. Next to no one knew about the businesses that Heath owned, and he planned to keep it that way. He had enough money in the bank to help his father out. Not that Pop would ever accept it.

"It's been a while since you were here." His father gave instructions to an employee and came around to face Heath. "You got your mother to drop you off, I assume?"

It took effort to not give a sarcastic response. *No, Pop, I hobbled two miles on foot. Literally. One foot.* "Yes, I insisted she bring me here while she finishes her errands. I didn't see any reason for her to come back twice. Mom said she'd be back to pick me up and take me home in a half hour."

Unlike his father, Mom had welcomed him home with tears in her eyes and the same comforting arms he remembered surrounding him as a child. He'd missed Mom over the years. Sadly, being away from his father had been more of a relief. It was a contrast that never balanced each other out. He'd called often, they'd spoken using video chat once a month, and Heath stayed far away from Clearwater. Mom always said she understood.

Now he was back. Pop's response to his visit at the store only served as a reminder that the ghosts of his past still hovered, waiting for the perfect moment to come floating out of the woodwork. It did no good to dwell on what happened between him and Raven, or the part his father had played in the whole thing.

~*~

Raven jabbed a spoon into her dish of ice cream. It was Saturday, and no matter what she did, she couldn't keep Heath out of her mind. Whenever she stepped outside of her house, she half expected to run into him. It was driving her crazy. Even now, sitting in one of Clearwater's favorite ice cream parlors, her eyes darted to the door every time it opened. This was ridiculous.

"What'd that ice cream ever do to you?"

The voice of Raven's best friend, Mandy Yarrow, drew Raven's gaze. Mandy was teasing, but there was a hint of concern on her face. She easily maneuvered eight-month-old Barry from one arm to the other. The little guy grunted as he tried to grab his mother's spoon.

Raven shrugged, scooped a large spoonful of chocolate fudge and shoved it into her mouth. She didn't have to answer questions if she was chewing, right?

Mandy dipped her spoon into the orange sherbet. It only made it halfway to Barry's mouth before the baby grabbed it and brought it the rest of the way. The moment that sherbet hit his tongue, he was ready for more.

"You'll have to watch him. He's got quite the sweet tooth." Barry always made Raven chuckle.

"Oh, don't I know it. He's all over eating pears and apples. But green beans? Not going to happen. He likes his meats, though, so that's something." Mandy gave her son a little more and then ate a large spoonful herself. "I'm serious. What's going on?"

There was no avoiding the question forever. Raven balanced her spoon across the cardboard bowl and frowned. "I saw Heath this week."

Mandy's brows rose. "Seriously?" She'd comforted Raven many times in the aftermath of the breakup. They'd talked a time or two about how he was back in town. "Where did you see him?"

"He walked into CRC. Fay assigned me to help with his physical therapy." She told Mandy about walking into the room and how awkward the whole thing was.

Sherbet forgotten, Mandy's free hand went to cover her mouth. "Wow. What are the odds?"

"I don't know, but I ought to buy a lottery ticket or something." Raven's voice betrayed her bitterness. Even the chocolate ice cream she normally loved didn't have its usual soothing effect on her. "I'll be seeing him twice a week for a while. I imagine he's trying to get enough therapy in so he can skip off to Cleveland again where he belongs." That type of injury could take up to eleven months to make a complete recovery. Raven couldn't fathom having to be around him that long.

"Have you talked to Fay? You shouldn't have to deal with this. If she'd known, I'm sure she wouldn't have assigned him to you in the first place."

Raven immediately shook her head. "I can handle it. It took years after he left before everyone I knew didn't constantly ask if we were getting back together. It's a nice change that none of my coworkers know anything about that mess, and I'd just as soon keep it that way." Raven paused and then smiled. "Besides, how many women get a legitimate reason to cause their ex pain through physical therapy?" She laughed. Although her friend laughed as well, it was clear Mandy could see right through Raven's tough-girl façade.

It didn't matter. Raven would do her job and get Heath back on his feet. Then he could hightail it back out of town. With any luck, it'd be another dozen years before he returned again. A girl could only hope.

She finished her ice cream and then held her arms out. "Okay, let me see that sweet boy of yours so you can eat in peace."

Mandy tossed her a look of thanks and handed Barry to her. Raven sat his padded bottom on the edge of the table facing her.

"Look at you, Barry. You've got orange sherbet all over your face. Much more, and someone might mistake you for an Oompa Loompa." She took a napkin, dipped it into her water, and wiped the sticky mess away. "There, now I can see your cute smile." Raven wrinkled her nose and made a face of her own that always got the baby giggling. Before long, those baby belly laughs filled the room and had several other patrons smiling as they listened.

Mandy reached over and patted her son on the back. "You're good with kids, Raven."

Raven shrugged. "It's because I refuse to grow up." She wrinkled her nose again and made another funny face at the baby. "Isn't that right, kid?" He laughed again. "See? Barry agrees." She played with him a few moments more. When she looked up again, she found Mandy watching her with that knowing look of hers. "What?"

"Nothing." Mandy painstakingly used her spoon to gather up the last remnants of her ice cream. "So how are things between you and Wade?" She made it sound casual.

That didn't fool Raven. She dug her keys out of her pocket and handed them to Barry who enthusiastically grabbed them from her. "I watched Longmire on Netflix Friday night while I ate cold pizza. I'm trying to decide between finishing off the pizza tonight or making myself a bowl of cereal." It was doubtful she'd be seeing her boyfriend of three years this weekend. Sure, she could've called him herself, but it'd been a busy week, and she'd hoped he would make the effort. Instead, she was avoiding her family and spending evenings alone.

Mandy's brows drew together. "So things aren't

going well?"

Raven shrugged. "We're lucky if we see each other once a week. He says work has been busy, and I get that. But I don't know." She swallowed hard as one of their more recent conversations replayed itself in her mind. She hadn't told Mandy about it, partly because she hadn't wanted to deal with it herself. "Wade's been talking about marriage."

Mandy waited for more. When Raven offered nothing, Mandy sighed. "Was he for or against it?"

The question brought one corner of Raven's mouth up in a half smile before it fell again. "Oh, he was a fan."

After she finished wiping her hands off on a napkin, Mandy took Barry back and settled him on her lap. "And you said…"

"I reminded Wade that we'd only known each other a few months." Raven winced. "So yeah, the fact he hasn't called is pretty telling." She couldn't blame Wade, though. If roles had been reversed, she would've backed off herself. Truthfully, the main thing she missed about Wade was the built-in excuse of having other plans, making it much easier to avoid her parents and sister. She didn't necessarily miss him. Guilt twisted in her stomach.

It was clear Mandy didn't need help reaching similar conclusions. "There's nothing wrong with telling him that." She paused. "You should come to our church, Raven. There are several great, single guys there. At least there's a good chance they'll have the same morals as you do."

Raven had been attending the same church since she was born, although the congregation contained mostly older individuals. If she tried to change churches now, she'd catch a lot of flak from her parents.

Raven gave her friend an apologetic look. Mandy, the true friend that she was, only smiled understandingly and changed the subject.

Raven enjoyed her career. She loved living in Clearwater and couldn't imagine moving anywhere else. She had amazing friends. But sometimes, while everyone else around her was falling in love, getting married, and having babies, her life seemed to be frozen in amber.

Chapter Three

Raven blinked at Fay, waiting for her boss to say she was joking or at least add more to her statement. The last thing Raven expected when she walked into work Monday morning was for Fay to ask if she should get Heath moved to another PT assistant. Not that Raven would object. "Why do you ask?"

"Mr. Shaw suggested there was history between you, and that a different assistant might be better." Fay watched her closely. "I wanted to check with you and see if *you* needed me to move things around."

Heath had the nerve to ask for a different assistant? Raven clenched a fist as she tried to keep her face neutral. "I hadn't seen him in over a decade. Any history we had is ancient by now."

Fay looked relieved. "So, you're okay with leaving the schedule as is?"

Part of Raven would be thrilled to switch and not deal with Heath. But another part of her didn't want to let him off the hook that easily. If he hadn't wanted to see the people he'd abandoned, maybe he should've gone elsewhere to recover from his injury. "Yes, I'm fine."

"That's great! Okay, that's all I needed." Fay flashed a happy smile and went on her way.

Raven had only moments before her first patient of the morning, seventeen-year-old April. The people Raven helped deserved her full attention. She shoved thoughts of Heath aside as she made final preparations to get the exam room ready. Five minutes later, she welcomed April along with her mother, Lilly, into the room. "How are you doing this week?"

April shrugged. Her unusually quiet temperament combined with the concern on April's face made Raven frown. She helped April up onto the table, got a chair for Lilly, and then pulled her own closer before sitting.

The poor girl had been through a lot. One of April's legs had been crushed in a car accident almost a year ago. She'd had several reconstructive surgeries and still had a long way to go in the therapy department to gain what everyone was hoping would be close to full use of her leg again. It was a lofty goal, but if anyone had the determination to make it happen, it was April.

For now, April wore a brace that stabilized her leg from the thigh down to the shin.

Raven nudged the girl's good leg with an elbow. "Come on, April, talk to me. I can't help if I don't know what's going on."

April glanced at her mother first and finally took a deep breath. "It feels like none of this makes a difference." Her voice broke, and Raven caught Lilly's chin quivering as she listened to her daughter. "It was okay when I first went back to school. But now, everyone's doing their own thing. It's my senior year, and I can't even keep up with my friends in the hallway much less go to my senior prom in a few weeks. No one's asked me, and I can't help but think it's because of my leg." She stared at the offending limb as though she'd pick it up and toss it away if she could. "I guess I'd hoped, when I started therapy months ago, that I'd walk on my own by now."

Raven's heart went out to the girl. She stood and withdrew the iPad from her pocket. "Come on, hop up."

April tossed her a questioning look but did as asked. With her cane in hand, she stood.

"Okay, now walk to the door and back." Raven used the iPad to record April's movements as the teen rolled her eyes and did as she was asked. When she returned, Raven helped her back up onto the table. "Give me a minute here." Raven went into the patient files and pulled up a second video. Once she had it, she went to sit on the table next to April. Lilly came closer. "Check this out. Do you remember when I recorded you walking across the room your first day here?"

April stared at the iPad and the frozen image of herself on the screen. "I'd forgotten about that."

Raven pushed play, and they watched as April slowly maneuvered her way across the room in crutches, pain etched into her face with every movement. When it had finished, Raven found the video she'd taken. "Now this one."

They watched as April used her cane to traverse the room in a fraction of the time. Not only that, but the girl stood straighter, and there was no evidence of pain in her posture.

When Raven glanced at the girl, she found tears rolling down her cheeks, mirroring that of her mother. "Honey, you have made huge progress. To go from where you were to what you're doing now is nothing short of a miracle. If any of your friends give you trouble, I'll be happy to tell them how much of a hero you truly are." Raven nudged the girl's shoulder with her own.

Even with the tears still falling, a smile transformed April's face.

"That's better." Raven hopped down and retrieved a box of tissues. She handed one to Lilly. "You have a strong, determined daughter who I know will eventually walk without a brace or cane one day." Then she handed a tissue to April. "And you don't give up, you hear? Feel free to come in any time you need a little kick in the tush to keep you moving."

April laughed then as she wiped her eyes and nose. "Thanks, Raven."

"You're welcome." Raven grabbed the small wastebasket and held it out for the soiled tissues.

"Now, let's get to work, shall we?"

Forty-five minutes later, she waved goodbye to a happy but tired teenager and her mother. More than satisfied with her patient's progress, Raven made notes in April's file. It wasn't until she'd hit save that she allowed thoughts of Heath to flood her mind again. The annoyance she'd felt this morning flared up again.

She sighed and reached for the small necklace she kept tucked into her shirt. Raven pulled it out now and looked at the heart with a cross etched into it. Mandy gave it to her last Christmas with a card that said she should look at it every time she needed a reminder of how much God loved her.

"I thought I'd forgiven Heath and put this all behind me," she whispered in the empty room. "Do me a favor, God? Help me get through this with my heart intact. Oh, and if You could keep me from killing him in the process, that would be great, too."

The moment Raven entered Heath's room at the Clearwater Rehabilitation Center on Tuesday, it was clear from her demeanor that Dr. Bright had informed her of his failed request to switch assistants. He suppressed a sigh. It was his own dumb fault. This was a small town, after all. Word got around. Of course a conversation with Raven's boss would filter down to Raven herself. He should have known better.

Well, if he thought she was all business last week,

it was nothing compared to the determined look in her eyes today. She asked him a list of questions and then went through the exercises one by one as if they were targets at the shooting range. No emotion. That's what bothered Heath the most. The indifference bothered him more than her anger would have.

He winced as pain radiated up his leg. He had to quit thinking about her and focus on what he was doing.

Raven noticed immediately. "We need to push your leg to heal, but if we're going too fast, let me know."

A hint of compassion flashed in her eyes before it disappeared. If Heath hadn't been looking at her then, he would've missed it. "No, it's good to push. No pain, no gain, right?" He gave her the smile that used to always earn him one in return.

Instead of a smile, she nodded once. "Okay. But I'm serious, speak up if we need to back off a little. We may have a whole recovery plan drawn up here, but no one knows your body and its limits like you do. It's important you listen to that."

Heath knew she was only doing her job and cautioning him on the amount of strain he was putting on his injured leg. Still, his spine straightened as he pushed his shoulders back. He had to get through this rigorous plan and back on his feet. His father had reminded him that morning about all that was at stake if he didn't get back on the field soon.

It gave Heath dual reasons to push through the

pain and recover as fast as possible: as much to escape the constant reminders from his father as playing football itself.

He watched Raven as she made a few notes on her iPad. Even when she was serious, a crease between her brows as she frowned, she was beautiful.

A conversation with his father during senior year replayed itself in Heath's head.

"Son, I know you like the girl. But she's just another pretty face." His father handed Heath his helmet on the sidelines of the football field. "Don't let a schoolboy crush destroy your chances of playing for the NFL."

Heath put the helmet on and then sought out his fiancée in the stands, a mix of pride and love on her face as her gaze connected with his. She'd waved when his father grabbed the mask of his helmet and brought Heath's head around.

"I'm serious, son. Don't screw up your future. Trust me, you'll regret it for the rest of your life."

Pop had been wrong about one thing. Raven hadn't been just another pretty face. His father had never taken their engagement seriously. But at the time, Heath couldn't imagine his life without her. This woman standing in front of him now was even more beautiful than the girl he knew in high school. Combine that with the maturity he saw in her, and the skill she had as a PT assistant, and it was clear his father had underestimated her.

Heath had underestimated her.

Regret wasn't exactly a foreign concept. He'd felt it every time he thought about Raven, his mom, or his hometown over the last dozen years. But right now, the guilt expanded in his chest with each breath, threatening to force its way out. He covered it by putting extra effort into the exercise he was supposed to be focusing on. Anything to deflect the emotion into something else, and that included pain.

"Good." Raven's voice brought Heath out of the mess of thoughts running wild in his head. "I think that's about it for today. Are you ready for the gym?"

"Yep." He appreciated that she made no move to help him. His muscles ached with the effort of the session.

She slipped her iPad into a pocket in her scrubs. The hallway was empty. Before she could walk away, Heath cleared his throat and interrupted her.

"Raven?" He waited for her to turn and face him before continuing. He tried to ignore the apprehension and curiosity in her eyes. "When I asked Dr. Bright to switch assistants, it had nothing to do with your skill as a physical therapist. You clearly know what you're doing here. I thought it might be easier on both of us." He cleared his throat again. "I should've left things alone. I hope it didn't cause problems with your boss."

She studied him for a moment. "No, it didn't cause any problems. I get it." Her gaze flickered from his face to the end of the hall and back. "This isn't what either of us would've chosen. But we've got a common goal—to get you back to Cleveland. If we focus on that…"

"…then hopefully we can leave the rest in the

past." Heath acknowledged the look of approval in her eyes, surprised by the mix of emotions that brought to him. Relief that she seemed more comfortable with their current situation. Yet sadness that him leaving town had so thoroughly ended all facets of their once-close relationship. He had no one to blame but himself, though. "You reap what you sow," as Mom would've said. Or, he thought wryly, his father would tell him, "You can't expect anyone else to handle the crap you've dealt."

Well, between trying to renew a relationship with his mom and getting through seeing Raven twice a week, he'd certainly created a quicksand of his own making. Now to get out of Clearwater before he sank completely.

Chapter Four

Raven adjusted the baseball cap on her head to shield her eyes from the setting Texas sun. The surrounding crowd roared as the Clearwater Raptors scored a touchdown. Raven balanced the hot dog she was eating on her lap and clapped along with them.

She hated football, but today it served its purpose as a distraction. She'd been working with Heath at the CRC for the past two weeks. They'd managed to keep the sessions completely professional, and that was the way Raven wanted it.

Unfortunately, it also looked like Heath would be in town longer than she'd first expected. He planned to stay until he was free of the boot. It made sense. If recovery continued at its current pace, she hoped that meant he'd be on his way back to Cleveland by the end of October. She tried to remind herself that was only a drop in the bucket compared to the last twelve years. Surely she could handle another four to six weeks.

Cheers brought Raven's focus back to the game.

Her twin sister, Rosie, leaned into Raven's shoulder and shouted, "Carl's done an amazing job with this team. Everyone's talking about how much of a difference his coaching has made." There was no missing the pride in her voice. In fact, no one in the general vicinity missed it.

Raven resisted the urge to roll her eyes. Instead, she smiled, nodded, and took another bite of her hot dog. She was happy for Rosie and Carl. The couple had been married a little over a year and expected their first baby—a girl—in two months. Rosie had the perfect life. Not that Raven was jealous. It just seemed like everything was handed to Rosie on a silver platter.

Rosie was born first—a whole whopping two minutes before Raven—but it'd been held over Raven's head all her life. Rosie was blessed with blonde hair that had later turned to a gorgeous dark blonde, while Raven had dark hair that was nearly black. According to her parents, that had been the deciding factor when it came to naming the twins. But the differences didn't stop there. Raven was the type of person who spoke her mind and got in trouble because of it. Rosie, on the other hand, always knew the right words to say. In other words, Rosie was the poster child her parents constantly compared Raven to.

If Raven had a dollar for every time her parents asked why she couldn't be more like her sister, she'd have a nice nest egg in the bank right now. Throw in that Rosie was married to a successful high school football coach and expecting their parents' first grandchild, and she could do no wrong.

Cue Raven. It didn't matter that she had a successful job as a PT assistant. In fact, her parents only saw her as someone who "fixed up" the local football heroes so they could return to a more important job.

Football. It was practically a religion in Texas, and Clearwater was no exception. Raven's family lived and breathed the sport.

Raven couldn't have cared less about football until she met Heath. The last thing she'd expected in high school was to fall in love with a running back. It wasn't until after he'd asked her out that she'd gone to her first high school football game.

Once they were dating, she never missed a game. A fact that had more than thrilled her parents. For once, their daughter, who preferred to stay home and read, was going to the games every Friday night.

Most families would be shocked if their eighteen-year-old daughter came home and announced she was engaged. But Raven's parents hadn't lectured her about being too young. Instead, they'd practically thrown a party, they were so excited.

When Heath first ended things between them, it was difficult for outsiders to know who was more upset: Raven or her parents.

Raven quit going to football games, and her parents found all kinds of ways to blame her for losing the love of her life. She was hoping she'd never have to set foot on a football field again, which worked for a while.

Then Rosie had to go and marry a high school football coach. Suddenly, Raven was a horrible person if she didn't go and support her brother-in-law at least a couple times a month.

At least there were hot dogs. She took another bite.

Her mom, Linda Weber, leaned in from the next row back and blocked the space between Raven and Rosie with her head. "You know your sister can't eat hot dogs while she's pregnant. Don't you think it's inconsiderate for you to do so while you're sitting right next to her?"

Raven's jaw would've dropped if she weren't such a lady and intent on chewing her food with her mouth closed. She knew Rosie was avoiding processed foods while pregnant and had nothing but respect for that decision. But she'd had no impressions that Rosie was even remotely bothered by Raven herself eating a hot dog. Good grief.

Raven swallowed her bite. "I just got off work, and a girl cannot live on nachos alone. It was this or go home and eat first. Then I'd miss half the game."

Throwing in football logic made it hard for her parents to argue. "Next time, we'll have you sit back here so it doesn't bother your sister."

The sister who had her hands clasped on her large belly as she watched her husband with a smile on her face. Yeah, she looked real bothered.

But Raven had learned long ago not to argue. "Sounds like a plan."

Mom nodded in satisfaction and leaned back again. Raven scratched her nose where some of Mom's hair had tickled her.

The crowd cheered about something Raven missed.

Rosie leaned closer. "Are you and Wade going to Kerrville with the team for their away game next week?"

"No, I don't think so. I haven't heard from Wade yet, but he'd mentioned going to see a show." Raven inwardly cringed at the half lie. Wade had commented about seeing a movie a month or so ago. They'd gone out once in the last two weeks, and it'd been weird. It was like the marriage topic was an elephant in the room that neither of them wanted to address. They'd eaten their meal and then gone their separate ways. Truthfully, every time they met, she expected him to break up with her. "Hopefully he'll make it to the next home game, though."

Rosie seemed satisfied with that.

Raven finished her hot dog and pulled her phone out. She checked texts and discovered it'd been over a week since she'd last heard from Wade. She typed out a short message.

"Hey. We haven't talked in a while. I hope all is well."

She sent it and then stared at the screen for several moments before slipping the phone into her pocket again.

Rosie grunted and placed a hand on one side of her belly. "Oh, this girl is using my bladder for a trampoline." She rubbed the spot affectionately. "Did I tell you we finally settled on a name?"

Raven sat up straighter and smiled at her sister's extended abdomen. She loved the idea of having a niece to spoil. "No! What is it? Oh, I know. You're naming her after me, aren't you? How kind!" She batted her eyelashes until Rosie smacked her on the arm.

"You are too funny." She gave Raven an amused look. "We're naming her Tilly Anne. With an 'e' of course."

"Of course." Raven used to tease Rosie about how often she watched Anne of Green Gables. Rosie swore she'd give her daughter the middle name of Anne one day. "It's a beautiful name." Raven couldn't wait to cuddle her little niece.

"Thanks!" Rosie beamed. "By the way, one of the ladies at the bank saw Heath the other day." She gave Raven a curious look. "Are you still his physical therapist?"

Their parents were seated in the row behind them. As soon as they heard Raven and Rosie talking about Heath, they were all ears. When they first found out he was going to the CRC for therapy, they'd been thrilled. But after giving Raven the third degree and getting nothing in return, the subject dropped. Now that Heath's name had come up in conversation again, they were nearly climbing into their daughters' laps.

Their father, Roy, put a hand on Raven's shoulder. "I always knew that boy would bounce back. Have you reconsidered the possibility of reconnecting with him?"

Raven didn't even fight the groan that escaped her throat. How many times did they have to go over this? The man she loved walked away from her and didn't even say hi for twelve years, and her dad wanted to welcome him back with open arms? Then again, her parents assumed she'd driven him away. If it was Rosie's boyfriend who'd left, Raven was certain things would've been different.

Rosie looked excited. "Maybe you can invite him to come to a home game. I know the boys on the team would be star-struck to have one of our own hometown heroes here to cheer them on."

Mom's voice sounded from behind. "What a great idea! I'm sure Raven will remember to ask him, Rosie. Anything we can do to bolster our team's enthusiasm is a good thing."

Raven rubbed her temple, her head pounding with a headache that seemed to intensify with each passing moment. If she had to listen to them talk about Heath for the rest of the game, she'd need at least an order of nachos and a double dose of Tylenol to go with it.

~*~

Heath stirred the pancake batter and then, using

a crutch to support his left leg, spooned some onto the hot griddle. His foot was steadily improving and didn't bother him nearly as much as it had even a week or two ago.

The sizzling sound plus the smell of bacon cooking in the skillet made his stomach growl. He missed these big Sunday breakfasts. He recalled many mornings watching cartoons on TV while his mother's amazing cooking filled the house with mouth-watering scents. They'd eat their big breakfast before going to second service at church.

It all seemed so long ago.

Today, his father sat at the dining room table as he read every word of the sports section of the newspaper. The cup of coffee he'd insisted on first thing that morning sat forgotten at his elbow. Meanwhile, Mom sipped at her orange juice and looked through the coupons.

Heath slid the spatula under one pancake and flipped it over without causing a mess. The first two pancakes hadn't fared so well. But then, he was out of practice. He didn't normally bother making himself a nice breakfast like this.

His father's paper lowered enough to reveal a pair of dark eyes watching him. "Son, you should sit and rest that leg of yours. Save your energy for therapy. Let your mother make breakfast."

Mom tossed him a disapproving look.

Heath flipped the other pancakes. "Mom made breakfast for me every Sunday growing up. The least I can do is make it for her today." When he winked at her, the smile she gave him made it all worthwhile. Even getting the flak from his father. "Besides, I need to earn my keep somehow."

His father lifted the paper to conceal his face again. "Get back on the field. That's repayment enough for me."

Mom cringed a little, but Heath gave her a reassuring smile. Truthfully, he'd been poking around town the last few weeks looking at real estate. He'd found the perfect place and planned to tell his parents this morning. Living with them the last month and a half was about all he could handle. Mom was great, but Pop made the whole thing way more difficult than it needed to be.

Heath added the cooked pancakes to the mangled ones on a nearby plate and spooned more batter onto the griddle.

By the time the meal was ready, Heath was glad to sit down again. He wasn't about to admit that to anyone else, though. He poured syrup over his pancakes and added some to his eggs. No doubt his father objected. The added sugars wouldn't be on what he'd consider a football-approved diet.

Mom lifted her fork. "This is wonderful, Heath. Thank you."

"You're welcome." He smiled. "I'm looking forward to going to church this morning. It'll be great to get out for a while." He hadn't ventured to church since he'd come back to Clearwater. At first, he thought he'd lie low, get through physical therapy, and get out of town again. But he'd already had buddies from high school stop by to say hello. When Heath dropped by the store for a while, he had a string of visitors there as well. In the end, he decided he may as well go back to church. Everyone seemed to know he was in Clearwater anyway.

Besides, he hadn't been going to church as regularly as he should be. Guilt twisted in his gut. *Sorry, God, that it took an injury like this for me to realize I was neglecting time with You.*

The three of them ate in relative silence for several minutes before Pop brought up therapy again. "You getting out of that boot soon?"

"Hopefully in the next month." Heath couldn't wait to be rid of the thing.

"Good. Then you can go back to that team of yours and show them how hard you're working to get back on the field." He speared a piece of pancake with his fork and popped it into his mouth.

Heath set his own fork down and took a deep breath. "Mom. Pop. I've decided to buy a place here in Clearwater."

Mom's face morphed into a huge grin, which was a direct contrast to the frown on his father's.

It was Pop who spoke first, a hint of anger in his voice. "You'd better not be talking early retirement."

"I'm not. But I need space here, and I think you do, too." He glanced at his mom. "I don't want this much time to pass before I see you again. I'll have a place to stay when I visit."

His words brought happy tears to Mom's eyes. He was doing this for her. For himself. He didn't think Pop would care either way, but the words that came out of his father's mouth shocked Heath.

"Raven." He spat out her name like a piece of rotten food. "You should have requested a different physical therapist weeks ago like I told you to." He turned his attention to Heath's mother. "He was never able to keep his head in the game when it came to that Weber girl."

Mom reached over and laid a comforting hand on Pop's arm. "Now, Gabe." But he only shifted away from her, crossing his arms in front of him.

Heath lost his appetite. "Don't you dare blame Raven for this. She has nothing to do with it—you made sure of that twelve years ago." He'd resented the way his father felt about Raven in high school, and apparently those feelings were closer to the surface than he realized. "I bought a new car I'm supposed to pick up tomorrow, Pop. And I purchased a house on the other side of town. I'm moving in this week. You know as well as I do that it's not healthy for either of us if I stay here. It'll give us both space until I can move back to Cleveland."

Pop stared at him, and Heath held his gaze without blinking until Mom spoke. "Raven's in a relationship and has been for months. Last I heard, they were serious about each other." She took a sip of her orange juice.

Heath straightened in his seat. He and Raven had steered clear of anything personal over the last few weeks. She'd never mentioned a significant other, and he'd refused to ask. He assumed the lack of a wedding ring meant she wasn't married, but apparently it was only a matter of time. "Really? I had no idea. That's great." Hopefully he'd put the right amount of interest in his voice.

"I guess he's a doctor over at the hospital. A renal specialist, I think. Pam at the hair salon knows Raven's mother."

For the first time that morning, his father relaxed a little. "That's good. Real good." He gave Heath another pointed look before returning to his breakfast.

A doctor. Wow. Yeah, she'd gone about as far away from dating a football player as she could. She deserved to be happy. To live her life. Wasn't that what they'd both been doing the last twelve years?

The unexpected twist of jealousy in Heath's chest only irritated him. He didn't care what Raven did in her spare time or who she dated.

Now how many times did he have to repeat that before he believed it himself?

Chapter Five

Raven tried to cover a yawn Tuesday morning as she waited for Chrissy to hand her a cup of coffee. The moment that cup touched her palm, Raven wrapped her hands around it and absorbed the warmth. Too bad she couldn't absorb the caffeine as easily.

When she'd talked to Rosie on Friday about Wade, she'd had no idea how different things would end up a couple days later. Why couldn't she go home and sleep the rest of the week away? Instead of rushing out like she normally would, Raven took a small sip and flinched as the hot liquid hit her lips and tongue.

"You okay?"

Raven looked up to find Chrissy watching her with concern. "What makes you think everything isn't?"

One corner of Chrissy's mouth pulled to the side, and she shot Raven that "Don't kid a kidder" look. "You want me to get you a mirror? Seriously, what's going on?"

Raven didn't want to talk about it, but then, she didn't want to go to work yet either. She sighed and sagged against the counter. "Wade broke up with me last night." There, she said it. That made it feel more official than the actual conversation with Wade had.

Chrissy looked over her shoulder. "Sal, I'm taking my ten." She got a nod of acknowledgment from her coworker, tossed a towel onto the counter, and led Raven to a corner table. "I'm so sorry, Raven. That stinks. What happened?"

"Nothing." When Chrissy looked doubtful, Raven continued. "I'm serious, nothing has happened for weeks. At first, I thought we were missing each other because of our schedules. He's always either at his office seeing patients or at the hospital, which I've understood and supported. I'd convinced myself that's why he hadn't called as much."

Looking back, Raven had suspected the breakup was coming. There were a handful of times she'd thought to go to the hospital to say hi or invite him to dinner. But every time, she'd worry she'd interrupt him or make him feel obligated. Those were all only excuses, though.

Raven told her friend as much. "What if I sabotaged this? What if it was all me? Wade is a great guy. Seriously, what woman wouldn't want a relationship with a surgeon who spends his time helping other people? Not to mention he's super sweet." She set her coffee on the table and let her head fall into her hands. "I'm defective, Chrissy."

The last thing Raven expected was to hear her friend laugh. Raven's head jerked up, and she shot Chrissy a look that insisted she explain herself.

Chrissy tried to stop laughing, held up her hand, and then burst into giggles again. "I'm so sorry, Raven," she said through short pants to get herself under control. "I wouldn't be laughing if what you said hadn't been so ridiculous." She reached for a napkin and tried to use it to fan her face. Purple strands of hair fluttered in the breeze. "You're right, Wade is a great guy."

Raven groaned. She knew she was letting him slip right through her fingers. What was wrong with her?

"But," Chrissy continued, "you are amazing, sweet, and anything but defective."

"What's your point, Chrissy?"

"It doesn't matter how perfect you guys were together if you weren't in love with each other."

Raven blinked at her friend. Love. She'd never been in love with Wade. The realization hit her so hard, it took several moments to digest the information. She had to guess that Wade had never been in love with her, either. Otherwise they wouldn't have been able to walk away from each other so easily. "You're right."

Chrissy crossed her arms in front of her and leaned back in her chair, a look of satisfaction on her face. "You're welcome."

Raven wadded up a napkin and tossed it across the table pegging, Chrissy right in the ear.

Chrissy picked it up off the floor and kept it out

of Raven's reach. "Is that the way to treat your best friend who also provides your caffeine fixes?"

Now it was Raven's turn to laugh. "Maybe not, but I can't let you go on thinking you're too perfect." She winked. Her mind returned to her recent break up and the smile on her face faded again. "The whole thing still stinks, though."

"Yeah, it does." Chrissy glanced at her watch and must have decided she still had another minute or two to talk. "Have you and Heath managed to get along without killing each other so far?"

Raven didn't particularly appreciate Heath coming up as a segue to their conversation about her failed love life. "We've been keeping it professional. It's all about his therapy and nothing else. Which is the way it should be."

"But you're getting along okay?"

"We're both working as hard as we can to get him back to Cleveland. Why he didn't see a PT there is beyond me." Enough about Heath. "So what's going on with you? Any hot dates lately?"

Chrissy snorted in a very unladylike fashion. "Um, no. You kidding? I'm pretty much here or at home." She leaned forward and lowered her voice. "The only interest I seem to get is from wackadoodles who think drawing suggestive images on a napkin along with their phone number is a good idea. Do they think anyone would call them back? If they're lucky, they'll get a restraining order one day."

Raven chuckled. "Are you serious?" Chrissy gave

her a look that said she was dead serious. "Wow, that's messed up. Come on, there has to be one handsome guy that frequents this place you'd happily go out with if given the chance."

Chrissy shrugged. "Maybe. But it would be completely unprofessional." She straightened in her seat. "Speaking of professional, I'd better get back to it."

"Yeah, I'd better go myself before I'm late." Raven smiled at her friend. "Thanks, Chrissy."

"You're welcome. Hang in there, huh?"

Raven lifted her cup of coffee in response. They both stood and went their separate ways.

Once in her car, Raven turned on the music and cranked up the volume to drown out all thoughts of both Wade and Heath. Belting out the chorus to "Carry On My Wayward Son" by Kansas certainly helped.

Once at work, she welcomed her first patient. Working kept her busy enough to keep the emotions of her failed romance from her head. Until Heath's appointment. With one hand on the doorknob, she took a deep breath. *Help me stay focused, God.*

She straightened her spine, turned the knob, and walked in. The sight of Heath sitting in the chair caused her heart to flip flop in her chest.

Until now, all the isometric exercises she'd been giving him had only required verbal instruction from her. Today, that would change.

She asked him the usual series of questions about his progress since their last session. Once she'd jotted down the answers, she took in a subtle breath. "Dr. Bright checked your incision on Thursday and everything looked great. Today we'll start scar mobilization therapy. Are you familiar with it?"

"Enough to hear it's not pleasant." He leaned against the back of the chair, his booted foot resting on the floor in front of him.

"That's true, although it helps a great deal in the long run. Once we can get that soft tissue loosened up, you'll experience less scar tissue and pain."

She'd hoped he would go back to Cleveland before they reached this point. Raven waited for Heath to remove his boot and then asked him to lie face down on the padded table. She placed a rolled towel beneath his leg just above his foot. "We'll start off with a gentle massage each session. After a week or two, we'll increase the intensity of the massage as the wound continues to heal."

She suddenly wondered if her hands were too cold. She slipped them into her pockets and kept them there as she explained what they would be working on. Hopefully it had been long enough to warm them up a little. Which bothered her because it wasn't something she normally worried about with the rest of her patients. It was all because of her conversation with Chrissy. *I need a vacation.* "Do you have any questions?"

Heath shook his head. "Nope. I'm ready to get started."

"All right." She withdrew her hands and made a point of not rubbing them together first. She narrated what she was doing as she slowly manipulated and stretched soft tissue around the scar. It was tight, but she'd seen worse. She felt Heath tense beneath her hands. Raven frowned. She'd joked about how not many people had the excuse to cause their ex physical pain and get away with it. But the truth was, she didn't like hurting him. He might have deserved a good punch to the stomach, but this was different.

"Let me know if this is too much. We want to work on decreasing the scar tissue, but we don't want to push things."

"No, no. This is fine." His voice sounded a little tight. He hesitated. "Look, I know we said we were keeping everything professional. Mom mentioned you've been dating a doctor and things were serious between you. I wanted to say I think it's great you found someone. I'm happy for you, Raven."

Really? After all these sessions, he had to mention Wade now, the day after they broke up? She didn't want to have this conversation. She realized she'd paused, her hands still resting on his calf. His muscles flexed beneath her palms, and she withdrew them as though she'd touched a hot stove. Yeah, nothing like talking about your ex-boyfriend with your ex-fiancé while you're holding his foot in your hands.

~*~

Heath bit back a groan. See, this was why he should've listened to his instincts and kept his mouth shut. This was why he'd told himself repeatedly that he needed to keep their conversations centered on his therapy and nothing more.

Raven stopped massaging the scar. She was still touching him, her slender fingers curved around his calf, but she'd frozen in place. A moment later, the pressure of her hands disappeared. "I…I had no idea your mom even knew anything about Wade."

So that was the guy's name. Mom said she couldn't remember. "Apparently, her hairdresser knows your mom, or something along those lines." He wanted to kick himself with his good foot for bringing this topic up at all. "I'm happy for you, Raven."

"Thanks." She uttered the word so softly, it was barely audible. Raven's warm hands touched his skin again, and he flinched as the sore tissue around his scar complained. Before long, she'd finished. He sat up and flexed his foot as he focused on her. She had her hair pulled up into a tight ponytail today, the end of it teasing one of her ears as it swung back and forth.

Heath swallowed hard as he remembered the many times he'd placed a kiss to that very ear. It seemed like a lifetime ago.

Raven cleared her throat, took a step away from the table, and looked at him. Uncertainty swirled in her brown eyes for a moment before she covered it with determination. "Wade and I broke up last night. I figure your mom will probably hear about it the next time she goes to the salon, so I may as well tell you." She shrugged as if it didn't matter, and her expression was neutral. Most people would assume the breakup didn't affect her much.

But even after twelve years, Heath could see she was fighting to produce that almost convincing smile. "I'm sorry, Raven." He paused. Part of him felt horrible for her. Yet, the tension that had gripped him since he'd heard about Raven's boyfriend eased a little. That only made him feel guilty. Letting this particular topic of conversation drop would be the smart thing to do. But before he stopped himself, more words came pouring out of his mouth. "I know it's none of my business, and I'm sure you have plenty of people you go to when something's bothering you. But if you need to talk… We're here for two hours a week, and I promise what's said in the therapy room stays in the therapy room." Heath's lame attempt at humor garnered a chuckle from her.

Raven shrugged. "That's not going to happen. It is what it is. We grew apart." The moment the words left her mouth, she reached for the iPad and made several notes. Her soft voice brought his attention back to her. "In case your mom wonders, you can tell her I'm doing okay. Truthfully, the decision to end our relationship was mutual."

This tentative side of Raven wasn't something Heath saw often. The whole time he knew her in high school, she'd been one of the most self-assured girls he'd ever known. "Still, it can't be easy."

"Oh, my parents will have a field day with this when they find out. It'll be one more sign of how I keep messing things up. They never even liked Wade. But he was a doctor and had money, so they made an exception." She paused. "You know how my parents were. They've changed little in the last twelve years."

"Yeah, the same with my father." There was a hint of frustration in his voice he hadn't meant to let through, and Raven picked up on it immediately. "If it were up to him, I'd be here eight hours a day, seven days a week. Whatever it takes to get me back on the field, because that's all that matters." He half expected her to agree with what his father might say, but Heath had shared enough about his family back in the day. She'd seen how his father was, too. He shouldn't be surprised to see the understanding and sadness in her eyes.

"I'm sorry. I figured your parents were thrilled to have you back after so long."

There was a slight emphasis on the last two words, and he couldn't blame her. Ignoring it, he shrugged. "Mom is. But Pop is still Pop. Life isn't complete without football in it." The dubious look on her face made him defensive. "There's a difference between enjoying the game—doing what you love for a living—and living for the game. A big difference." The words came out harsher than he'd intended. But he didn't appreciate even the most remote comparison between himself and his father. They were nothing alike. Heath had always loved football, but his father had almost ruined that for him, too.

Raven released a sigh. "It's too bad everything

with family has to be so complicated, isn't it?"

"Yeah, it sure is."

They were both silent for several moments. Heath shifted on the table. His foot throbbed, and they hadn't even started the rest of the exercises.

"You going to be okay?"

"Sure." Heath ran a hand through his hair. "Working at the gym is bound to make it feel better."

She gave a half-hearted laugh at his sarcasm. "I wouldn't count on it." Raven nodded toward his foot. "Seriously, though. You're making great progress. Hopefully you'll be out of that boot by the end of October and free to head back to Cleveland. At least you won't have to listen to your father try to push you any longer."

"Isn't that the truth? Things haven't been easy with him." He paused. "I bought a house on the north side. I'm moving in today or tomorrow."

He thought Raven would drop her device the way she pivoted toward him. "What?"

The look of shock with a splash of panic bothered Heath. He raced to clarify. "I can't handle living in that house with him for another day. Besides, it'll give me a place to stay when I come back to visit Mom. If being back here has taught me anything, it's that I don't want to stay away as long next time."

Raven was studying him, and he couldn't quite read her face. A heartbeat or two passed before she spoke. "I'm sure your mom would be thrilled if you visited from time to time." She glanced at the clock.

"We'd better get moving on the isometrics before we run out of time."

It was all business again. But for Heath, something had changed. Every other appointment, he couldn't wait to put space between himself and Raven when he headed to the gym.

Today, when it came time to leave the room, part of him wanted to linger.

Chapter Six

When Raven showed a new patient to the gym late Wednesday morning, the last person she expected to see there was Heath. After she answered her patient's questions, the sight of Heath lifting weights made her pause. Her instinct was to walk out before he saw her, but the therapist in her couldn't. What was he doing here? Before she knew it, she was moving in his direction.

He sat up on the weight bench with a groan as she approached, his eyes widening in surprise. "Hey."

"Hi." Raven crossed her arms in front of her. "What are you doing here?" She nodded toward his injured foot. "You should be careful to not push too hard."

"Why? You worried about me?" Heath's smile transformed into a grin.

The same grin that used to make her pulse thrum. Apparently, she had yet to develop an immunity to it.

She raised her brows at him. "I'm serious, Heath."

"Yeah, I know." His smile fell away. "I was hoping to get moved into my new place yesterday, but there was a delay. I should be set for tomorrow, but I have way too much anxious energy to sit around and wait. So I came here." He glanced at his watch. "How about I take a quick shower and we go grab some lunch?"

Raven stared at him. Sure, they'd had an almost normal conversation yesterday during his session. But that didn't mean they were suddenly friends again. It was a big leap to go from one conversation to eating together.

When she didn't answer right away, he added, "You do still eat lunch, right?"

Despite everything, a small laugh bubbled to the surface. "Yes, I still eat lunch." She should tell him no and keep their interactions firmly in the professional realm. But the hopeful look on his face, combined with the reassuring knowledge he'd leave again in a few weeks, stopped her. Finally, she nodded. "I take my lunch in twenty minutes."

"I'll find you in fifteen," he promised, his smile returning.

Raven raised a hand in acknowledgment and went to finish some paperwork. The whole time, she kept kicking herself for agreeing to go to lunch. There wasn't any way out of it short of sneaking out of the CRC before he returned, and she wouldn't stoop that low.

Before long, they were standing on the sidewalk out front deciding where to eat. They settled on a sandwich shop a block away. Heath used his thumb to point toward the parking lot behind him. "I hope you don't mind if we drive."

Raven glanced at his foot. "Of course not."

"Come on, I'll give you a ride. No sense in taking two cars."

She wanted to object and take her own vehicle. Instead, she followed him to a shiny black Ford F350. It looked brand new. "You just get this?"

"Yep." He ran a hand along the sleek surface of the passenger door. "One blessing about messing up my left foot: I can still drive while wearing this stupid boot." He pulled the door open and motioned for her to climb inside.

Once at the sandwich shop, they ordered and then found a place to sit in one corner of the dining area. Raven took a sip of her sweet tea. This was the first time she'd had a chance to sit down all day. She relaxed against the back of her chair and let out a sigh.

Heath observed her from across the table. "Are Wednesdays usually this busy for you?"

"If it weren't for Fay's scheduled mandatory lunch breaks, I'd probably skip it most of the time."

"Then I'm glad she insists. Everyone needs a break." He nodded toward her tea. "I expected you to order coffee. Are you not addicted to the stuff like you used to be?"

Raven chuckled. "I prefer to call it a serious

hobby." She lifted her cup and took another sip. "I'll get some coffee this afternoon. There's a place I prefer, and I'll need the caffeine fix to get through the rest of the day. I take it you still don't drink it?"

"I have a cup most mornings now."

That was a surprise. There was something in his eyes that suggested there was a story behind that statement. But someone from the sandwich shop brought their food to the table, and they both focused on their meals for a while. Three times over the next half hour, someone Raven didn't know stopped by to tell Heath hello or shake his hand.

"I had no idea you still knew so many people here in town."

"I don't recognize most of them." He shrugged as if it were no big deal.

"I don't think I could get used to that." It was like sitting with a movie star. The interruptions from his fans were getting on her nerves.

Heath took a bite of his dill pickle. "It doesn't bother me most of the time." His cell phone rang, and he glanced at the screen.

"Do you need to get that?"

"Nah." He silenced the phone. "It's Benny, one of my teammates. I'll call him back later this afternoon."

Raven hadn't even considered that Heath might be staying in touch with his team while he was in Clearwater. It made sense, though. Was he wishing he were back in Cleveland right now?

She pushed that thought from her mind. Last night, Raven's family had reminded her to invite Heath to one of the home games. Now seemed as good a time as any. "Look, my sister wanted me to ask you something. You are free to say no. In fact, I encourage it." She wiped her hands off on the napkin she was holding. "Rosie's husband is the coach for the Raptors. They were wondering if you might go by one home game and say hi to the kids. Maybe encourage them a little." She held a hand up. "There, I've officially asked. Like I said, don't feel pressured."

"Wow, so Rosie married a coach. I'll bet your family is over the moon." He polished off the rest of the dill pickle.

"You aren't kidding. As far as they're concerned, at least one of their daughters didn't screw up her life." She tried to sound aloof. He had no idea what all had happened once he left after high school. "Anyway, I know they'll ask me about it at the game tomorrow, and now I can say I've passed along the invitation."

The corners of Heath's mouth lifted in amusement. "You go to the high school football games?"

For some reason, the fact he found humor in it annoyed her. She sat up straighter and gave him a firm glare. "It's expected."

"It can't be that bad. Surely they'd understand if you didn't want to go."

"They think my biggest failure was not convincing you to take me with you when you left.

Football is a frequent reminder I could do without. I wouldn't go to another game if I could get away with it." Raven dropped her wadded-up napkin onto the table next to her plate. "But it's worth it to avoid the guilt of not being there to support my sister and her family."

~*~

Heath stared at Raven as her words hung in the air between them. What? He'd regretted how he left Clearwater—how he'd left her—but never once did he blame her. That her parents had was ridiculous.

"I had no idea, Raven."

"It doesn't matter anymore. I go to the games when I can, put a smile on my face, and pretend I don't hate that blasted sport."

The way she spat out those last two words made Heath's heart ache. Back when they were together, she'd never missed a game. She'd been on the sidelines and cheered as much as anyone else. In fact, it'd been her smiling face that had given him so much drive when he'd been out there on the field.

That she hated it now was his fault. He'd known his decision had hurt her, but he hadn't allowed himself to consider all the ramifications. And she'd been dealing with it for a dozen years. He knew then he'd make it to the next high school home game. If nothing else, at least her family might give her credit for that and get off her case for a while. He owed it to her. "I'll check the schedule when I get to my parents' house and make it out there soon."

"Thank you."

"You're welcome." He watched as she pinched off some ham from her sandwich and put it on her tongue. She'd only eaten half of her lunch, and it didn't look like she would eat any more. "Not hungry?"

"I'll wrap this up and eat it for dinner." Her gaze roamed the dining area before it focused on him again. "Sorry, I shouldn't complain so much. Rosie and Carl are perfect together. Their first baby girl is due the first week of November. I'm truly happy for them, and it's given my parents something to focus on, too, which is never a bad thing. It's just…" She stopped, and her cheeks grew pink.

"It's just they've been on your case since I got back."

She shrugged. "The past always rears its ugly head."

Heath needed to shift the topic away from football. "So you're going to be an aunt, huh? Looking forward to it?"

"You know, I really am. I'll be one of those aunts that my niece comes to when she has a fight with her parents so she doesn't get into trouble. I want to be the fun aunt that's always making her laugh."

"You'll be great at it, and she'll be lucky to have you."

"I appreciate that." Raven looked like she was about to say something else before she clamped her lips together. Even though she was now finishing the last of her cheddar and sour cream potato chips, the question shined in her eyes.

"Out with it, Raven."

She shrugged. "Well, you know about my breakup with Wade and how my parents blame me for being single. What about you? I half expected there to be a Mrs. Heath Shaw nursing you back to health."

Her question was more than fair, but it didn't mean it was an easy one to answer. "I've dated some. I guess I haven't found the right person who can forgive my crazy work schedule." He winked, hoping that was answer enough. Truthfully, no girl he met could compare to Raven. He'd given his heart to her in high school, and when he'd moved away, he'd neglected to take it with him. She didn't need to know that, though. "Besides, can you imagine me bringing a girl home to meet my father? If she wasn't scared off before, that'd finish the job."

"He is a force to be reckoned with. I never knew how your mom put up with him."

"All I can figure is they balance each other. Opposites attract and all that." A look at his watch told him Raven's lunch hour was nearly up. They needed to get going as much as he'd rather stay there and keep talking. "I'll go get you a to-go box for the rest of your sandwich."

By the time he returned to their table, Raven had wrapped her sandwich up in the paper that lined the basket. She took the container from him, placed her sandwich inside, and grabbed her bag. They walked back to his truck.

He pulled up to the curb outside of the CRC. "Don't work too hard, okay?"

Raven pointed to his leg. "You go home and put your feet up."

"I will. Scout's honor."

She gave a quick nod and turned to open the truck door. Heath reached out and gently grasped her upper arm before she could leave. When she swiveled to look at him, her eyes full of questions, he swallowed hard.

"I never should've walked away, Raven. I'm sorry. And I'm sorry people hold it over your head. It isn't right."

Raven seemed surprised by his apology. She leaned away from him, reached for the door handle, and paused. "But you did leave, Heath. You made your decision and life went on." After opening the door, she got out and turned. "It couldn't have been just you, though. I obviously made it easy for you to walk away."

With a frown on her face that nearly broke Heath's heart, Raven raised a hand in a half-hearted wave and disappeared into the building.

He squeezed his forehead with one hand. The discomfort didn't even come close to erasing that look on her face from his memory. It was one more image to add to his mental photo album that reminded him of the many times he'd disappointed her. If only she had a clue how difficult it'd been to leave her behind.

He didn't feel like going back to his parents' house yet. Instead, he pulled into a nearby lot, parked his vehicle, and dialed Benny's number.

"Hey, Heath. What's up, man?"

"Not much. Sorry I missed your call. What are you up to?"

There was a lot of noise in the background. "Crushing it at the gym. Hang on a sec." More muffled sounds and then Benny's voice again. "Guys, it's Heath."

A roar of voices rumbled through the line as everyone hollered greetings. It was impossible to tell what anyone was saying, but it still made Heath grin. He missed working out and playing with the guys.

Benny announced his return with a laugh. "You hear that?"

"I heard it. Tell the guys not to worry. I'll be back to set the pace for y'all soon."

That earned Heath a guffaw. "Right, man. You talk to Coach lately?"

"It's been a week or two. I'm keeping him up to date on my progress." Heath frowned. Knowing his teammates were continuing with their rigorous training only made him feel like he was falling behind. How hard would it be to jump back in once he returned?

"Good. Well, quit slacking and get back here, huh?" Someone spoke to Benny. "I've got to run. Talk to you later?"

"You bet." The call ended, and Heath tossed his phone onto the passenger seat.

With a heavy sigh, he checked for traffic, and headed to his parents' house. What he wouldn't give to be going to his own home this afternoon. Maybe there he could forget his career was on the line and pretend to not think about Raven in peace.

Chapter Seven

Raven didn't dare mention a word about inviting Heath to a home football game. After the end of their lunch yesterday, and the awkward therapy session today, she seriously doubted he'd make the effort. No, it was better that her family think she hadn't bothered asking him and be disappointed than to face the inevitable unending questions when he didn't appear.

She was so convinced Heath wouldn't come near the field that it took a second and then a third look before she realized he was standing at the bottom of the bleachers. Her breath hitched as her heart pounded against her ribs. Great. These football games were hard enough with the memories from another life. She didn't need the source of those memories to walk back onto the scene now.

It's only for one game, Raven. Chin up. Pretend like nothing has changed.

A squeal behind her announced that Rosie had

spotted Heath. Within moments, she was holding her very pregnant belly and side-stepping down the row of seats to the walkway. Raven bit back a moan as Rosie made her way to the field where she hooked arms with Carl as they greeted Heath.

A hand gently patted Raven's shoulder, and she turned to see her dad standing behind her. "You came through. I'm proud of you."

Proud of her for inviting Heath to the game to support the high school boys? She ought to be stunned that he said it at all. In fact, she should write this momentous occasion on her calendar to celebrate every year. Unfortunately, it didn't mean that much when he hadn't even said those words when she graduated high school or finished her degree to become a physical therapist assistant.

All Raven could do was stare numbly at the crowd growing around Heath. He shook hands and clapped shoulders with a wide smile on his face. Across the way, Heath's father sat where he did every Friday, pride etched into his features.

It was as if they'd been transported to a time twelve years ago. Apparently, no one remembered or cared that Heath had disappeared without so much as an update or a single visit back home. How many months had Raven waited, hoping he'd come back again? The flood of emotions she'd felt back then began to pummel her heart yet again.

She still remembered every tiny thing about their last conversation.

It was semi-dark on the sidelines of the field long after the game had ended. Heath had put his hands on her shoulders, a mix of determination and sadness in his eyes.

"Raven, it's not fair of me to take you away from Clearwater. From your family and friends. You'll be miserable in Portland if you go with me. And I can't stay here with you." He'd run his hands from her shoulders to her wrists. "You deserve someone who can give you everything you've ever wanted. Who can love you more selflessly than I can."

Tears had raced each other down Raven's cheeks, though she'd hardly noticed them. "We can make this work, Heath. You said you wanted to get married. To raise a family together." She'd swallowed hard, searching for the words that might convince him to change his mind. "I love you."

"I love you, too. I probably always will. But this is the way it needs to be." His brows drew together as he clasped her hands in his. "I'm sorry."

Raven had pulled her hands away, slipped the engagement ring from her finger, and slammed it into his palm. "Yeah. Me, too." Her eyes flashed as she wrapped her arms around herself and took a step back.

He'd stared at the ring for several moments before putting it in his pocket, turning, and walking away from her. From them.

Raven shook herself to try and dislodge the memory from her mind. For months, she suffered from the daily heartache of hoping she'd walk around the corner to find Heath standing there, waiting for her. Until she finally wised up and realized she might never see him again unless it was on television.

Raven forgot she was staring at Heath and the crowd of fans until his gaze shifted and locked with hers. His smile slipped long enough for her to notice before he had it back into place.

Ugh! Even after being mad at him all these years, that smile still made her heart stutter. How fair was that?

Her parents were talking in the row behind her and focused in on what they were saying.

"This is a good thing, right?" There was no missing Mom's voice. "Maybe she'll come to her senses and beg him to stay this time."

"Now, Linda. You know that boy's going back to Cleveland. Maybe she'll follow him there."

Tears pricked the back of Raven's eyelids, and she blinked them away. She couldn't do this. The field held too many memories she was trying to keep at bay as it was without her parents bringing up the past and trying to "fix" her future.

She jumped to her feet and half turned toward them. "You know, I'm not feeling well this evening. It's probably allergies, but we've had a couple people at the CRC come down with something. I think I'll go home and get some rest. I wouldn't want to be too sick to help Rosie out with the homecoming committee."

Her parents looked like they might object until she threw in the homecoming committee. There was no messing with that. Mom finally nodded, stood, and placed a kiss to her forehead.

"No fever, thank goodness. Get some sleep,

honey. We'll talk to you tomorrow."

"Okay. Love you guys."

Dad patted her on the back as she walked past them and out of the stifling row of seats. She kept her eyes on her feet as she traversed the stairs to the cement below. Even the thought of a hot dog made her stomach roll. Cereal for dinner sounded just fine tonight, if she bothered to eat anything at all. Going to bed early sounded even better.

She'd nearly made it to the parking lot when someone gently grasped her hand and stopped her escape. She turned to find Heath standing there, concern in his eyes.

"Hey, where are you going in such a hurry?"

"I'm not in a hurry."

He chuckled. "I practically had to run to catch up to you. Not as easy these days as it used to be." He held his left foot up.

For a moment, Raven felt bad. But he didn't have to run. He didn't have to come out here at all. The flash of guilt dissipated. "If your foot's bothering you, maybe you're the one who should go home again." Even as the words left her lips, Raven knew they sounded much harsher than they should have. After all, she was the one who'd extended the invitation to come in the first place.

The frown on his face combined with the flash of confusion in his eyes. "Say the word, Raven, and I'll leave."

She glanced around and found they were

somehow miraculously alone. "Look, I'm not feeling great and decided to head home and start my weekend early. You should go back. I know the boys are thrilled to have you here." She forced a small smile. "Your fans are waiting."

Instead of turning to leave, he kept studying her face. She didn't know how much longer she could maintain this attempt at civility. Not when she realized they were standing under the tree where he'd kissed her silly after his first win on the team. Suddenly all the kisses they'd shared while sitting on the bleachers or waiting on the sidelines flooded her memory. Or the time they'd lain on the grass after the game, staring up at the stars, as they talked about their future. A future together.

What a joke.

The moment Heath saw Raven leaving the field, he could tell something was wrong. Her shoulders were stiff, her back straight, and her chin down. Raven rarely exuded anything but confidence. His brain warned him to let her go, but his heart clenched and convinced him to go after her.

He excused himself for a moment and caught up, his foot protesting even with the use of his crutches. When she turned to face him, it was clear she was upset. There was an underlying edge when she said his fans were waiting for him.

It'd surprised him that so many people had rushed to greet him when he arrived. Sure, he played football for the NFL, but he hadn't been back to Clearwater in so long, he'd half expected no one to recognize him or care he'd returned. But fans? He wasn't sure he'd go that far.

"I don't think it's like that. Half the people I'm talking to are people I knew back in high school. Or their parents. You're reading way too much into this."

Yeah, that was the wrong thing to say.

Raven's eyes widened. "You're kidding me, right?" She motioned toward the bleachers filled with eager high school football fans. "You're like the prodigal hometown hero who has finally returned. My parents are talking about ways to make me come to my senses and take you back. Then you come here and everyone's welcoming you with open arms. It's like you'd left for college last week or something." Pink tinged her cheeks as she spoke.

Heath couldn't tell if she was embarrassed or angry or both. "Maybe you should be upset with your parents. I've never known you to carry a grudge like this." His voice sounded as incredulous as he felt.

She held both hands out to her sides. "I'm amazed that you can come back, and it's as if you'd never left. As if you'd never forgotten about them in the first place."

Heath's back stiffened. He glanced back at the field, relieved no one was close enough to hear their conversation. "I left for college, Raven. It's what most of us kids did back then."

"No." She put her hands on her hips, the anger on her face morphing into sadness. "You walked away from your town, your family." She swallowed hard. "You walked away from me. And instead of visiting like every other college kid does, you disappeared, leaving me to deal with the fallout."

He'd seen no alternative back then. The thought of coming back to Clearwater and seeing Raven with another man had plagued him for years. The longer he was away, the easier things were. Why couldn't she understand that?

Raven motioned toward the bleachers. "Your fans may welcome you with open arms and are happy to forget the past, but it's not that easy for me."

Heath placed a hand on each of her shoulders and waited until she lifted her eyes to meet his. The mix of emotions there left him guessing at which one was closest to the surface. "I'm sorry if my coming back to Clearwater has made it harder on you. If it's any consolation, it hasn't been a cake walk for me, either." He paused, searching for the right words. "Leaving this place—leaving you—was the hardest thing I'd ever done. I couldn't come back. And every year that passed made it that much harder."

Raven searched his face a moment before finally shaking her head and stepping away from him. "You could've come home any time, Heath. You *chose* not to." Her anger melted away, leaving only a look of disappointment in its wake.

"That's where you're wrong." He folded his arms in front of him. "I might have returned to Clearwater, but I could never come home again. The moment I left, I no longer had one here."

"Whose fault was that?" She pierced him with a glare before turning and walking toward the parking lot.

The disappointment on her face was like a knife slicing into Heath's heart. He could handle almost anything she dished out to him. But he'd been fighting to keep from disappointing people all his life. It's why he'd first tried out for the football team: To make his father happy. He hadn't expected to love the game himself.

If that's how she felt, then there wasn't a thing he could do to change her mind. In fact, this made his life easier. She'd written him off. There was no need for him to try and mend any part of the friendship they once had. That ought to make him feel better, but it didn't.

Raven was wrong about one thing. He couldn't have come home before now. Her response tonight only proved that fact.

He watched her for a moment longer before rotating toward the field and walking back. There wasn't a thing he could do to fix what Raven thought of him. But at least he could make sure he didn't disappoint the boys on the football team. Encouraging them was something he *could* do right now.

The boys on the team sat riveted to his every

word as he told them about life in Cleveland and shared the pearls of wisdom he'd learned from playing high school football himself. Raven's brother-in-law, Carl Law, seemed like a great guy that the boys respected. They were lucky to have him for a coach.

When Carl invited Heath to join them on the sidelines, the boys on the team cheered so loudly, Heath couldn't say no. By the time the game was over, he'd said hello to more people than he could count, signed autographs, and somehow got wrangled into helping with homecoming. Rosie promised to call or text him with the details in the next couple of days.

Late that night, he collapsed on the futon in his new house and stared at the ceiling. His entire left leg ached from the thigh down to his toes. It was a good thing he had two days off before going back to therapy on Monday.

Raven.

It was nearly midnight. Was she at home sleeping peacefully? Or awake battling the slew of conflicting emotions like he was? For the first time in years, he wished they had the kind of relationship where he felt free to call her. He even wished he had a friend he could talk to about all of this. But truthfully, even though he considered some of his teammates to be friends, he'd never been as close to anyone as he'd been to Raven.

Chapter Eight

This past week had been ridiculous, awkward, and long. After their heated conversation last Friday, Raven expected their therapy sessions to be weird. It was as if both she and Heath were on autopilot and only spoke when necessary. The ease with which they had worked together in previous weeks was gone. Even when it felt strained before, at least they could laugh or visit about their week.

This... This was miserable.

Thankfully, Raven finally made it to the weekend. She dreaded going to the away game tonight. Normally, she'd much rather stay at home and watch a movie than make the thirty-minute drive. But this was all part of Raven's master plan.

Once Rosie had the baby, Raven would suggest a family dinner once a week and then bow out of going to football games. With that in mind, she could handle a few more torturous games if it meant an end was finally in sight.

She had no intention of riding over with her parents, though. Taking her own car and reserving the right to go home early was a much better idea.

Later that evening, she settled into a seat next to her mom with a hot dog in one hand and a soft pretzel in the other.

Mom looked at the food with disapproval. "Really, Raven? How are you going to keep your figure when you keep eating like that every Friday? Please tell me you live on salads the rest of the week."

Fridays were Raven's junk food days, but Mom didn't need to know that. She shrugged, held up the pretzel, and grinned. "We seriously need to carry these at our concession stand back home." Then she took an exaggerated bite. Yep, she'd remember to suggest it next week. The Clearwater High School had been offering only nachos, hot dogs, and sodas for years now. It was time they expanded a little.

"Hey, stranger."

Raven looked up to find Chrissy plopping down in the seat beside her.

"Hey! I don't remember the last time you came to a football game."

Chrissy shrugged and rotated the silver ring on her right thumb. "I usually work Fridays. But one of my co-workers owed me a favor and swapped shifts with me this week. Figured I ought to get out and show a little Clearwater pride." She pointed to Raven's hot dog. "And I need to get me one of those."

Raven handed the hot dog over along with packets of ketchup, mustard, and mayonnaise. "It's on me." She'd only gotten both because she knew it'd drive her mom nuts. Sure enough, Mom nodded approvingly.

"You sure?" Chrissy took it and immediately squeezed a packet of mustard all over the dog. "Thanks." She took a bite. "Oh yeah, that's what I'm talking about."

Mom touched Raven's arm. "Honey, I see someone I want to visit with for a while. Do you mind?"

Raven shook her head. "It's fine."

Dad was somewhere else, and Rosie had disappeared for a while, too. At the moment, Raven was happy to relax and visit with Chrissy. "I'm glad I came tonight. I almost didn't." If it'd been a local game, she would've stayed home. The odds Heath would show up at another event were small, but she didn't want to risk it. Going to the game tonight gave her leeway with her family next week if she decided to bail.

"I'm glad you did, too." Chrissy motioned to the field where players were warming up. "I played clarinet in the band, but I never got into football." Chrissy had grown up in Utah and only moved to Clearwater five years ago. "Football was important, but not quite as big in Utah as it is here."

"No doubt. It's practically a religion in Texas." Raven rolled her eyes, and they both laughed. She finished her pretzel and was wadding up the paper sleeve it'd come in when something on the edge of the field caught her eye. She squinted against the bright sun getting lower on the horizon. It couldn't be.

There stood Heath, visiting with the crowd of people around him as if he belonged at the game. Raven released a heavy sigh and sagged against the back of her chair.

"What? What's wrong?"

"That's Heath down there with his flock of adoring fans."

"Ooooh, let me see." Chrissy didn't hesitate to stand, shield her eyes, and get a good look. She only sat when Raven grabbed the hem of her shirt and tugged her back into her seat. "You failed to mention he's crazy good-looking."

While they'd talked about Heath a lot, Raven had never shown her friend a picture of him. Truthfully, she never imagined the two of them would meet.

"I didn't see the point."

"So you agree he's hot?" Chrissy waggled her eyebrows, her eyes twinkling with mischief.

Raven nudged her friend with an elbow. Of course he was hot. If anything, he was even more so now than he was back in high school. His lanky form had filled out, the muscles in his upper arms bulging against the sleeves of his shirt every time he flexed them. It was no wonder there was a handful of women chatting with him, all clearly enamored.

"It doesn't matter," Raven muttered under her breath. "He'll leave again in a few weeks and everything here will return to normal." This right here was why she insisted on bringing her own car. She'd be heading back to Clearwater before the game ended. What she needed was a change in topic. "Are you volunteering to help with the float this year?"

"Yep." Chrissy polished off the rest of her hot dog and got a tissue out of her bag to wipe her hands. "Clearwater Coffee is donating drinks for all the volunteers tomorrow. I'm bringing those in, and then I'll stay to help for a while. You, too?"

"I'll be there." Under silent protest. Raven had been roped into helping for the second year in a row. "And I'm stoked you're bringing coffee. You'll be the most popular volunteer." Knowing her favorite coffee would be waiting for her when she volunteered tomorrow helped a little.

Chrissy smiled and nodded. Her gaze shifted, and her eyes widened. "Looks like you've got company."

Raven glanced up to find Heath walking up the steps to their row, his gaze on her. Great, what did he want?

~*~

Heath picked his way toward Raven. If the look on her face was any indication, she wished he'd trip and fall back down the stairs to the field below. On the other hand, the friend she sat with watched him curiously. He was pretty sure he hadn't met her before. It would be hard to forget someone with such colorful hair or the amount of jewelry this woman wore.

He'd seen the two visiting earlier and wondered if Raven was telling her friend all about the issues between them. Until Raven laughed. She'd seemed so at ease, there was no way he was the topic of conversation.

Now Raven looked uncomfortable, which bothered him as much as if she'd been angry to see him. "I'm sorry to interrupt. Rosie found me below and wanted me to let you know she's sitting on the sidelines today. She told me her back is hurting, and she didn't want to walk up the stairs."

Raven's brows furrowed. "Is she okay? Maybe I should find her and see if there's anything I can do to help."

Heath shook his head. "She assured me she was fine and said you should just enjoy the game." He glanced at the people milling below. "I'd forgotten how nice this field is." He'd played here many times in high school. In fact, he remembered one time assisting in a touchdown and looking toward the stands to find young Raven standing and cheering for him. She'd seemed so happy back then. A stark contrast to the way she looked now. "Anyway, I wanted to pass along the information."

Okay, now this was awkward. He ought to leave, but he didn't know where to go. Find another seat, he supposed.

"Sit down, Heath." Raven pushed the seat of the chair down next to her.

She sounded aggravated, but when Heath looked at her, there was no way to tell what she was thinking. "You sure?"

Raven shrugged. "Your call."

Well, he couldn't very well leave now. He settled into the seat beside her, his elbow brushing hers as they met on the shared armrest. Electricity traveled up his arm and straight to his chest.

Raven jerked hers away. Had she felt it, too? Or was she so repulsed, she couldn't stand the thought of touching him?

She cleared her throat. "Oh, this is my friend, Chrissy. Chrissy, meet Heath. An old friend from high school."

Ouch.

Heath reached in front of Raven to shake Chrissy's hand. "It's nice to meet you."

"You, too." Chrissy gave him a genuine smile.

He ignored the uncomfortable look on Raven's face. "What do you do for a living? Or are you a football groupie?"

Chrissy chuckled at that. "No, not a groupie. I think this game is the first I've attended this season." She nudged Raven's shoulder with her own. "I work at Clearwater Coffee. I'm the one who enables Raven's caffeine addiction."

Raven smiled. "I should look into getting stock in that place," she admitted. "But I promise I didn't become your friend because you work at a coffee shop."

She and Chrissy laughed.

"I'll have to check the place out." Heath made a mental note. Raven had always been particular about her coffee, so if she liked Clearwater Coffee, it had to be decent. He'd have to plan what time he went by. If it were in the morning or at lunch, there was a good chance he could run into Raven. The thought held a lot more appeal than it ought to, and that surprised Heath. Spending time with Raven was the last thing he needed to do. He shouldn't even be sitting with her in semi-awkward silence. Thankfully, Chrissy leaned forward to see around Raven and asked another question.

"I heard about your foot. How's physical therapy going?"

Heath lifted his boot. "It's going well. I've made more progress than I'd hoped." Which was true. Between the treatment plan Dr. Bright had drawn up and the therapy Raven had been providing, it was clear coming back for rehabilitation had been the right decision. There was no doubt Raven excelled at her job. He wouldn't hesitate to recommend CRC to others who might need it.

Raven straightened and waved to someone at the base of the bleachers. With a smile, she jumped to her feet and said, "I'll be right back."

Heath watched as she traversed the steps and gave someone a hug. The girl looked to be in high school and talked animatedly with Raven.

"That's April," Chrissy volunteered. "She goes to CRC, too. Raven's been working with her for months.

The doctors originally told April she'd never walk again. Raven promised she'd have her dancing at homecoming, even if it was with some help."

The two continued to visit and even though Heath couldn't hear a word that was spoken, his heart swelled with pride. This was what Raven was made to do. She had a way with people, and he could see the admiration and respect in the girl's eyes.

"I'll bet Raven will do it, too."

Chrissy nodded. "She doesn't make a promise she can't keep."

Those words made Heath pause. It's true, Raven had always valued truth and honesty. Back in the day, if he'd only told her about all the pressure Pop had been putting on him, maybe things would've been different. Instead, he'd hidden many of his reasons for leaving. He frowned. Raven had deserved much better than that.

A few moments later, Rosie approached Raven. They talked, and Raven patted her sister on the back. She handed over her car keys before jogging up the stairs and into the row in front of Chrissy and Heath. "Hey, guys. Rosie said she isn't feeling well. I'm going to take her home." She focused on her friend. "Sorry to duck out on you so fast. We need to go watch a movie and chill or something."

"Absolutely. I'll text you with my next days off." She made a shooing motion with her hand. "Go take care of Rosie. Tell her I hope she feels better soon."

"Will do." Raven finally turned from Chrissy to

Heath. "Enjoy the game. See you on Tuesday."

"Yeah. Be careful driving back." He watched as Raven grabbed her bag from under her chair, gave them a wave, and walked away. He couldn't take his eyes off her until she'd disappeared from sight. Only then did he realize he'd been staring and muffled a sigh.

Chrissy smacked the arm of her chair with her palm and stood. "Well, I'm going to go mingle a little. It's rare I get to escape the coffee shop on a Friday evening. It was nice to meet you, Heath."

Heath stood. "You, too." Once she'd left, he regained his seat.

Hopefully Rosie was okay. He'd noticed she seemed exceptionally tired when she'd found him earlier to remind him of his promise to volunteer. It was good Raven took her home.

Unfortunately, it meant he'd be watching the game alone. The unexpected wave of disappointment was nearly as annoying as this tension between him and Raven.

Chapter Nine

Rosie grabbed Raven's arm. "Oh! And don't forget to ask Nell to contact the florist on Fourth Street. They were supposed to get back to us on flower donations a week ago."

Raven nodded as she jotted notes in the small notebook she held. Rosie had been talking a mile a minute the last half hour, and the list of things Raven had to accomplish once she arrived at the school later that afternoon was getting longer and longer.

Volunteering to put the float together on the Saturdays leading up to homecoming was one thing. Taking over Rosie's job of organizing everyone was something else entirely. Not that she blamed Rosie. Her poor sister had fallen asleep immediately after getting home last night. When she woke up this morning, she'd started cramping. With the baby's due date still nearly a month away, everyone insisted Rosie put her feet up until her doctor's appointment Monday morning. Raven couldn't agree more. If managing things today helped her sister, then Raven could handle it for one day.

When Rosie tried to add another item to the list, Raven reached over and put a hand on her shoulder. "This isn't resting. This is stressing, which is the last thing you need. I've got it covered. And I promise I'll talk to Nell or call you if I have any questions."

"Okay." Rosie's nose wrinkled. "Are you sure you don't mind staying for the whole five hours? Everyone's supposed to take shifts. I feel bad you'll be there the whole time."

"It'll be fine. I've got this. You stay here, bake that niece of mine a little longer, and try to get some rest."

Raven had to answer that same question at least two more times before she headed for the high school and left her sister to take a nap.

The parking lot outside the oversized garage was busy. Every year, the garage behind the school was used to house the parade float as it was built. For the students taking shop, the float itself was one of their largest projects. Everyone else who volunteered helped to place flowers and other details on the intricate design the art students came up with.

It was a huge project that always brought out the best in the school and the surrounding community. She and Heath had volunteered together two years in a row back in high school. Raven sighed. Once again, memories she didn't want to deal with fought their way to the surface.

Raven shouldn't have worried, though. The moment she stepped foot in the garage, there was no time to think about anything but the job at hand. Between people asking for directions and the to-do list she was slowly making her way through, the first two hours went by like a flash.

She'd just gotten great news from Nell about the florist when a voice spoke from behind her right shoulder.

"Where can I help?"

That voice caused goosebumps to pepper her skin as her stomach erupted in flutters. She turned slowly to find Heath standing there looking uncomfortable. "What are you doing here?"

He put one hand against the back of his neck. "Rosie and Carl asked if I'd be willing to help out this year. I figured I may as well since it's better than sitting around my empty house. At least I can do good here. I didn't realize you were volunteering, though, much less in charge." He jabbed his thumb in the air toward the door. "I can leave. Just say the word."

Raven looked around at the crowd of people. The turnout had been great, but experience reminded her they could always use more volunteers. Rosie would be thrilled to know Heath had taken the time to come by. Raven's feelings about Heath had nothing to do with what was going on here. Besides, hopefully Rosie would get some rest and take over again next weekend.

Heath was watching her closely, and Raven finally shook her head. "You should stay. We can use anyone who has the time to spare. I'm not supposed to be in charge, but Rosie was tired last night, and we were worried about her being on her feet all day. This is temporary." Normally, she would've volunteered the first two hours and then made her escape. That meant she might not have run into Heath at all if things hadn't changed.

It would've been so much easier if she'd missed seeing him entirely. But the continuing flutters in her stomach along with the blood pounding in her ears suggested otherwise. There was a part of Raven that was happy he was here. Why did things always have to be complicated when it came to Heath?

She lifted her notebook and turned to the page outlining the different volunteer stations. "Did Rosie put you in a specific group?"

"I told her I could help with construction or painting, but I'm up for whatever they need." He cleared his throat. "It's kind of you to take this over. I hope Rosie knows what a great sister she has."

His words surprised her. She raised her chin and looked at him, half expecting to see he was teasing. But everything about his expression radiated sincerity.

She gave him a quick bob of her head and willed herself not to blush. She turned her attention back to the notebook. "I think they could use an extra hand over in construction."

"Sure. I'll go check in with them." He gave her a

wink and disappeared into the crowd.

Raven glanced through the list of volunteers Rosie had given her. Sure enough, Heath's name was there in black and white. How hadn't she seen it before? It said Heath had committed to be there from two to four o'clock. With all he was going through in physical therapy, it was kind of him to agree to help here, too.

She couldn't stop the small smile that tugged at the corners of her lips. With a groan, she rolled her eyes at herself. What was it about Heath that made her feel like a silly schoolgirl? She had a job to do today, and so did he. With any luck, they might not even cross paths again.

~*~

Except for his recovering foot, Heath was in great shape. Regular checkups with the team doctor had assured him he was a specimen of good health. He worked out constantly to keep up with the rigors of playing professional football. Even still, lifting lumber and swinging a hammer for hours used muscles he'd forgotten he possessed.

He flexed his right arm and shook it out. Building this float may be a lot of work, but it took him back to his junior year when he'd been one of the students on the building committee. By that time, he and Raven had been seeing each other for over a year. They'd volunteered because it not only helped the school, it gave them yet another excuse to spend time with each other.

Heath's gaze scanned the thinning crowd in the garage. He finally spotted Raven near a row of tables where women and girls were arranging everything they'd need to decorate the float once it was painted. He glanced at his watch. It was half past four. He'd stayed later than he'd intended, but he had a feeling Raven had been here since the beginning. Her shoulders drooped a little, and she ran a hand over her face before continuing her conversation.

Everything was wrapping up on the construction end. A couple guys were cleaning up and encouraged everyone else to head home.

Heath shook several of the men's hands. Carl came up and gave him a big smile. "Thank you for helping today. The construction came along faster this year than it usually does."

"It wasn't a problem. You've got a great group of people here."

Carl looked around him and nodded. "Yeah, we do." He tipped his head toward Raven. "I'm so thankful Raven convinced Rosie to stay home and rest. I had my concerns months ago when Rosie volunteered to organize everything this close to her due date. But that's one thing about my wife, she doesn't know when to quit. Most of the time that's a good quality to have…"

"…except when it's not." Apparently the sisters were a lot alike when it came to that trait.

"Exactly."

"Well, I'll be praying that baby stays put for a while longer, and that Rosie can get some rest. I'll be back next Saturday."

"I appreciate that, man. On both counts. Get on out of here and have a good rest of your weekend."

Heath gave him a wave and headed for the coffee station set up along one wall. He grabbed a cup and fixed it the way Raven used to like it. Hopefully her tastes hadn't changed too much.

People were filing out of the garage fast when he found her alone writing things down in that notebook of hers. "Here." He handed her the cup of coffee. "From what I've seen, you need this. It's only lukewarm by now, but it's better than nothing."

Raven looked up in surprise but didn't hesitate to accept the cup. "Oh, yes. Thank you." She took a tentative sip, her eyes widening. "You remembered."

He found more satisfaction in the pleased expression on her face than he should have. It was a stupid cup of coffee. Remembering the way she liked it shouldn't be that big of a deal.

Except it apparently was for both of them.

She sagged against a wall and sighed. "Wow, there's no way Rosie could've done this. In fact, I don't think she should be doing this next week, either. Now to see if I can convince her to hand the whole thing over to Nell or me." She grimaced.

"It's going to be you, isn't it?" He chuckled.

"Yeah, probably so." She held the cup to her

mouth and smiled behind it. "But Rosie has a good excuse this time, so I'll let her slide." She took another sip, her eyes closing in bliss.

Heath watched her dark lashes as they rested against her creamy skin. In this moment, she looked at peace. How many times had he studied her beautiful face and admired the way her eyelashes fluttered as he moved in to kiss her? Remembering the way she felt in his arms gave him an insanely strong need to reach for her now. He took a step back as her eyes opened again.

He cleared his throat. "Are you going to stay the whole five hours every Saturday?"

"Probably. Speaking of which, weren't you supposed to go home an hour ago?"

He shrugged. "I guess I wasn't in a hurry to leave." He hadn't wanted to let go of the nostalgia of working here with Raven.

Raven studied him as though she were trying to see the meaning behind his words. She was so intent he had to keep himself from shifting his weight in response. "Well, I think we're about done for the day. I suggest we get out of here before something else comes up." She drained the rest of her coffee and tossed the cup in a nearby trash can.

Heath waited while she checked in with a couple of people and then followed her to the nearly empty parking lot. She stopped at her vehicle and turned to face him. "Thanks for taking the time to help out today. We appreciate it."

"Of course." Now that they were outside in the

sunlight, something sparkled in her hair and on her cheek. He chuckled. "Looks like you got up close and personal with some glitter."

"What?" She scrubbed at her head with both hands and then laughed as glitter fell to the ground at her feet. "Oh, I'm going to find that for days, aren't I?"

"Probably." He grinned. His eyes went to her lips and then the little scar he still didn't recognize. He pointed to the corner of his own mouth. "What happened?"

She covered the left half of her mouth self-consciously, her cheeks taking on a pretty pink hue. "It was so stupid. We'd had a bad storm two or three years ago. Ice then snow with more freezing rain on top. It wasn't pretty." Raven rubbed at the white scar before letting her hand drop to her side. "I was walking into work and slipped on the sidewalk. When I tried to catch myself on a metal display, I managed to pull it down on top of me. I ended up with this lovely reminder of how less-than-graceful I am on ice."

Heath flinched. "Ouch."

"It bled like a stuck pig. Of course it looked worse with several drops hitting the snow. One of my coworkers drove me to the hospital. It only needed two stitches, but it felt like it took forever to heal. Unfortunately, it also left the scar."

"I think it gives you character. Makes it look like you were in a fight on the hockey rink or something." He winked at her. When she laughed, his heart rate sped up. "Seriously, though. I'm sorry that happened."

Raven shrugged. "I lived." A few pieces of glitter fell from her hair onto her bare arm. She brushed it away with a laugh.

"You've got a piece on your face, too." As if his hand had a mind of its own, he reached out to gently brush away a speck of gold glitter on her cheek. He froze the moment he touched her skin. A section of hair brushed against his hand. Heath swept it up and deposited it behind her ear before letting his thumb linger on her cheek.

Raven took a sharp breath, her lips parting. Did she have any idea how tempted he was to lean forward and kiss her right now? He took a small step closer, placing him near enough to inhale the scent of her hair and feel her breath on his chin as she looked up at him.

The sound of a car door slamming burst the bubble that had momentarily held them captive. Heath's arm dropped as relief and disappointment hit him in equal measure.

Raven shifted away from him. She pressed her palms to her forehead and groaned. When she lowered them again, the softness in her eyes earlier was replaced with frustration. "This," she pointed to herself and then to him, "can't happen."

"Raven, we—"

"No." She turned to unlock her car and open the door. "We were over a long time ago. In fact, there is no 'we.' Not anymore." She slid behind the wheel. "See you at therapy, Heath." With that, she slammed the door and drove away.

Heath stared at the tail lights until they disappeared. He formed a fist and dug his fingertips into his palm. The exhaustion from his work on the float evaporated, and all he wanted to do was hit the field. The problem was, he wasn't sure what bothered him more: that Raven had so easily dismissed any mention of the two of them in one sentence, or that he was tempted to chase her down and prove her wrong.

Chapter Ten

It didn't matter how hard Raven stared at the sermon notes on the screen above the pulpit, or how desperately she tried to focus on what the pastor was saying, her mind kept going back to that parking lot yesterday. She'd almost kissed Heath. Or more like he'd almost kissed her. Honestly, she wasn't even sure now. What mattered was she'd nearly made a colossal mistake.

Good grief, how many times had she daydreamed about him returning, pulling her into his arms, and kissing her like he used to? How often had she hoped he'd walk back into her life and admit they belonged together?

Now that the first part of that daydream had come true, she didn't know what to do. Sure, he'd bought a house and a new vehicle. But for someone who had a lot of money now, it probably didn't even make a dent in his bank account. He was leaving again.

Who knew when, or if, he'd come back?

It didn't matter how much she'd wanted him to kiss her yesterday. It didn't matter how handsome he was, or that she was drawn to him like before. This. Couldn't. Happen. *Fool me once, shame on you. Fool me twice, shame on me.* She refused to repeat history.

Raven groaned. *Okay, God. I could use a little help down here. I don't suppose You have an extra-large dose of will power lying around, do You?* She could picture God looking at her with raised eyebrows. *Yeah, I know. I know.* She'd had to pray many, many times over the years about letting go of the situation with Heath so she could move forward with her life. She'd had to stop thinking of him all the time or obsessing about all the reasons he'd walked away from her. From them.

This was no different. She needed to keep her feelings buried where they belonged. If she didn't do it, her heart would be trampled, and the pieces lost in the dust he'd leave behind.

Mom elbowed Raven in the ribs and mouthed, "Are you okay?"

Raven nodded. She had to pull herself together. She looked to the row in front of them, keenly aware of the empty spot where her sister and Carl usually sat. Rosie and the baby's health were much more important than any petty emotional breakdown Raven was having over her ex. With that in mind, she pushed thoughts of Heath aside and prayed for her family.

By the time Tuesday morning came around, Raven was feeling more confident about herself and keeping her emotions contained behind a brick wall in her heart. Hopefully Heath would come to his senses as well, and they could both walk away from this little trip down memory lane.

That afternoon, she rested her hand on the door to the room where she knew Heath was waiting, straightened her spine, and pushed it open. She found him sitting in the chair waiting for her. He seemed happy to see her, although there was a hint of uncertainty in his eyes. "Hey."

"Hi." She gave him a smile, trying her best to act like she would with any other patient. "How's your day going so far?"

"Good. I had Benny mail a box of clothing, and it arrived this morning. It's nice to have more than three shirts to choose from." He looked down at the red one he was wearing now.

"I'll bet." She leaned against the counter and crossed her arms. "I have more good news. You've progressed to where you only need one physical therapy session per week. If it works out well for you, we'll continue every Tuesday and drop the Thursday session."

That seemed to surprise him, but he nodded. "Sure, that sounds good."

"Great. We'll continue with that for the rest of the month. With any luck at all, you'll be out of that boot and on your way back to Cleveland the first week of November." Raven was happy she managed to sound professional. She made notes about the change in weekly schedule before glancing up at Heath. The look on his face made her wonder if she'd been *too* professional.

He said nothing, though. He took his spot on the table and Raven began the scar mobilization therapy. She worked in silence until he spoke, his deep voice startling her.

"Where did you go to school?"

Raven paused, her hands resting on his leg. "What?"

Heath raised himself up on his forearms and looked at her over his shoulder. "After high school, where did you go to college to pursue a job in physical therapy?"

Before Heath had broken their engagement, Raven had planned to go to Portland State University for a degree in health sciences. At the time, she hadn't known what kind of a job to pursue. Honestly, she'd figured they'd get married before he graduated and then she would stay home once they started a family. A career hadn't been part of her long-term plan.

Once they broke up, the last thing she wanted to do was leave her hometown and put herself in a position where she might run into Heath regularly. With Clearwater Rehabilitation Center doing so well, she figured becoming a physical therapist assistant would almost guarantee her a job.

Raven forced herself to continue massaging the soft tissues around Heath's scar. "I went to Concorde in San Antonio."

"Close enough to come home every weekend if you'd wanted to."

She nodded, although he couldn't see the silent response. "It worked out well. And Fay—Dr. Bright—has been great." She finished with her work on his scar and the surrounding area.

Heath sat up again. "While working out in the gym, I've heard several patients sing your praises. Apparently, you're the PT assistant people hope to get." He got down from the table and began isometrics. "I always knew you'd do well in a field where you focused on helping people."

That surprised Raven. She wasn't sure how to respond. "It's been a very rewarding experience. I feel like I'm making a difference here." That was something she'd desperately needed back when she'd first started at CRC. Now she couldn't imagine working anywhere else.

She busied herself with notes in his chart while he worked on the exercises. A moment later, Heath cupped Raven's elbow with one hand, the touch sending shivers down her spine. "I'm glad you're happy, Raven." He paused. "I hate how weird things are between us right now. I'm sorry." With one side of his mouth pulled to the side, he gave her elbow a gentle squeeze and let his hand drop.

She rubbed the area where her skin still tingled.

He was sorry. For what? Their almost kiss the day before? Or because they both knew he was leaving again?

~*~

Once Heath left CRC, he headed to his father's store. The parking lot in front was busy. When Heath entered, it seemed his father still had a lot of regular business. So why wasn't he maintaining the store? It was a question he'd puzzled over several times since his last visit.

Heath greeted people he knew as he made his way through the shop. He found Pop in the office at the back. As soon as his father finished a phone call, he ushered Heath inside.

"What are you doing here, son?"

"I thought I'd see how things were going. Looks like business is good out there."

"It is." He closed a ledger and slid it into a file cabinet drawer before locking it. "How'd therapy go today?" The tone of his voice suggested he wasn't interested in the topic.

"Just fine." Heath's thoughts centered on Raven. "I'm down to one session a week now."

His father nodded absently as he shuffled through scraps of paper on the desk in front of him.

Heath had gone over a dozen different ways to ask his father if he needed monetary help with the store. But for every one of them, he knew it would damage his father's pride. So he'd come up with a different approach. "I was wondering if you needed an extra hand around the store."

His father tossed the pen onto the desk a little harder than necessary. "I don't need your help here. You worry about getting yourself back on the field where you belong." The lines along the corners of his mouth deepened as he clamped his lips together.

"Right. Well, I'll get out of your hair and let you get back to work." He turned and was nearly through the office door when his father spoke behind him.

"Heath."

"Yeah?"

Pop handed him a small fabric grocery bag. "I promised your mother I'd bring these by. Since you've got nothing else to do today, I'd appreciate it if you'd drop them off for her." He gave Heath the bag and went back to work.

Heath hefted the weight of the bag in his left hand and left the store. First irritation, then sadness, settled in his chest as he drove the short distance to his parents' home.

He knocked on the door. The moment Mom answered, her smile faded. She noted the bag he was carrying. "What did he do?"

Heath put his free arm around her shoulders. "It's fine, Mom. Just the same old stuff. Don't worry about it."

She shook her head. "Don't play games with me, Heath. What did your father do?"

Heath put the bag in the kitchen and then sank onto the couch in the living room. Mom joined him. She knew him too well, and he finally told her what happened at the store. "I've noticed how much the place needs paint and a few repairs. I thought I could work with Pop for the next few weeks, you know? Maybe help spruce the place up a little."

Mom closed her eyes briefly before opening them again. "Your father is who he is, for better or worse." She paused. "I'm going to tell you something, but you have to promise to never let your father know."

Her serious tone of voice had Heath sitting up straighter. "Okay."

"Your father had some heart trouble five years ago." The moment she saw the shock on his face, she held up a hand to stop him. "Now, I know what you're thinking. At the time, we didn't want to worry you. It didn't seem to be a big deal. But six months later, your dad went into the hospital with chest pains. They ended up having to do a double bypass. He's been on medication ever since."

Heath leapt to his feet as fast as he could and turned to face Mom. "And you never thought to tell me? I would've been here in a flat minute had I known." How could they keep something this important from him? Anger boiled as he wondered what had possessed them to keep the whole thing a secret.

Mom frowned, her eyes filled with sadness. "I know, Heath. It was wrong not to tell you. But your father is a very proud man. The doctor told me it was imperative that your father have as little stress in his life as possible, and your father made me promise. I chose to respect that."

The resentment Heath felt for his father shifted and included his mom as well. He lowered himself to the coffee table and scrubbed a hand across his face. "This family is seriously messed up. You know that, right?" He looked at his mom, not even trying to disguise his emotions. "What if something had happened to Pop on the operating table?" His voice broke. "I'd regret not being there for the rest of my life."

Mom's chin quivered, and her eyes swam with tears. "I'm sorry, Heath," she said, her voice barely above a whisper.

He wanted to stay angry at her. But the truth was, Pop had been so difficult for so long. Heath knew it was hard for Mom to walk the line between them. He shifted to sit next to her on the couch again and pulled her into a hug. "I get it, Mom. I'm not happy with the decision you made, but I get it." He felt her sigh and placed a kiss to the top of her head. "I take it the medical expenses have been rough."

Mom nodded. "We're making it, and we'll be okay. But there hasn't been much left to pour back into the store. And you know how your father is. He considers his heart his weakness. So every day when he goes to that store and sees the repairs that need to be made, they remind him of why he can't take care of them. He's way too proud to ask for help."

Heath knew that was true. "Do me a favor? If I

ever get like that, you be sure to smack some sense into me, okay?"

Mom smiled. "I'll remember that." She released a lungful of air. "Your father has a lot of regrets in his life, and instead of facing them, he projects them onto others."

When Heath looked at his mom, the grief on her face squeezed his heart. "I don't believe for a second you were ever one of those regrets."

She nodded. "Neither were you." She sighed. "But I learned long ago there's not a thing I can say to change how he feels." Mom shrugged. "Thanks for bringing the groceries by."

"You're welcome. I'd have you over to my new place for dinner, but all I've got for furniture is a futon, a table, and some paper plates. I think you'd like the house, though."

"I'm sure I would. Maybe next time you're in town." She looked hopeful. "How's Raven doing?"

One of Heath's eyebrows rose in surprise. That was a swerve in topics. "Okay. Why's that?"

"Oh, I heard she and her boyfriend broke up. I hated to hear that." Except the tone in her voice suggested otherwise.

Heath gave her a stern look. "I'd heard, and she seems to be doing okay."

"That's wonderful." She paused. "Maybe it's not a coincidence that you're back in town, and she's single again…" Her voice trailed off.

"Mom." There was no way she could miss the

warning tone of his voice. "When I left, I didn't just burn that bridge, I blew it up."

"It's just... You've been in love with that girl since you were kids."

"A lot can change in twelve years, Mom."

"You're right. But can you honestly tell me you no longer have feelings for Raven?" When he didn't answer right away, she smiled in satisfaction. "Maybe this is your second chance. Have you spoken with Raven?"

Heath thought about their near kiss the other night, and a small spark of hope came to life. But then Raven's words nearly put it back out again. "No. But she's made it clear how she feels."

Mom placed a hand on one of his. "I know your father has always had a certain path he's expected you to follow. But the most important thing you can do is to pursue what makes *you* happy." She patted his hand and stood. "I'll go make you a sandwich, I'm sure you're starving after therapy. Come on in when you're ready."

He nodded but stayed seated.

Do what made him happy? Isn't that what he'd been doing all along? He enjoyed playing football. Not every guy got to play a game he loved for a living.

His father had harped about regrets and making sure Heath didn't make the same mistakes he had. Heath had grown up determined to not let regrets and bitterness rule his life. He didn't want to be like his father in another ten or twenty years.

But wasn't he on that track now? His thoughts shifted to Raven. Leaving her behind had been the big regret that had haunted him since he was eighteen. Instead of fading, those feelings had only intensified since he'd returned to Clearwater.

His father had drilled into his head back then that Heath couldn't have a career in football and have Raven by his side. Maybe it was time to prove to Pop—and himself—that he'd been wrong.

What would it take to prove to *her* that Heath wanted to be a part of her life? It was high time he figured that out.

Chapter Eleven

Raven's phone pinged first thing Thursday morning with a text message from Rosie. Every time her sister texted, Raven was sure her sister was going into labor. Thankfully, the cramping Rosie had experienced calmed down, and she was up and around again. At least she was trying to take things easy, for which they were all thankful.

Raven tapped the message to open it.

"Don't forget the birthday party on Sunday. 1 p.m. Dress nice!"

As if Raven could forget their joint thirty-first birthday.

Her parents had thrown a party for her and Rosie every year since they were four or five. Dad always served steaks, hamburgers, or something else that he could cook on the large grill outside. Mom made an amazing dessert that everyone wowed over. In the end, the guests had fun and walked away impressed which was exactly what her parents wanted.

Best of all, Mom and Dad were on their best behavior, which meant Raven didn't have to suffer through the normal contrasts between her and Rosie. Compared to the rest of the year, it was like a mini vacation.

Mom liked to plan parties while pretending to be an impartial parent, and Raven liked to eat. It was a win-win.

She texted back. *"I'll be there with bells on."*

The birthday party would be a great distraction from her life right now. The thought cheered her up as she got into her car and headed for Clearwater Coffee for her morning caffeine fix.

This would be the first Thursday in weeks where she didn't have to worry about seeing Heath. Her stress levels had dropped only to be replaced by disappointment. Raven chose to ignore it as she found a parking space and walked into the coffee shop. The tantalizing scents of coffee and pastries filled her nostrils. She didn't normally grab breakfast, but today, a scone might be in order.

Raven only had eyes for the counter up ahead where she could place her order, so when someone spoke to her from a table on her right, it startled her. She turned and stared. What was Heath doing here?

He stood. "I was hoping I could buy you a coffee this morning."

She took in the table where he'd been sitting. It was empty. How long had he been waiting for her?

Stalker much? A million questions filled her mind, but all she said was, "No, thank you. I need to grab something quick and get to work."

There was no missing the flash of disappointment in his eyes before he'd schooled his features. "In that case…" He motioned for her to get in line ahead of him.

Raven preceded him, but now all she could think about was that he stood right behind her. When it was her turn to order, Chrissy noticed them both and gave Raven a quizzical look. Raven returned it with a subtle shrug and hoped her friend would say nothing. She placed her usual coffee order, added a scone, and went to sit in a chair nearby while she waited.

She watched as Heath ordered a coffee. Once he'd paid for it, he joined her in the chair next to hers.

This whole thing was weird. Was Raven the only one who got that? She looked at him out of the corner of her eye. "I still can't believe you drink coffee now. You didn't tell me you'd sustained a head injury during your football career." After all, he'd disliked coffee enough that Raven had always eaten a mint between when she drank it and kissed him.

Really? Did all memories linked to Heath have to lead to kissing?

Heath chuckled. "No head injury." He paused long enough to make Raven question whether he was going to say more. Finally, he took a deep breath. "I drank it when I started school at PSU."

Despite trying to play it cool, Raven turned her

head to look at him. "Why?"

He shifted to face her. "Because it reminded me of you."

"Raven! Your order's up."

Raven jumped at the sound of Chrissy's voice and hurried to the counter to claim her coffee and scone. Chrissy leaned forward and whispered, "What's he doing here?"

"I don't know," Raven returned in a fierce whisper of her own. "I think I've entered an alternate universe or something."

"Text me later."

Raven nodded. She was tempted to leave but couldn't be quite that rude. Instead, she turned to Heath. "Have a good day."

She'd barely exited the coffee shop when she heard Heath's voice behind her. "Wait, Raven." He caught up to her, his crutch under his left arm and a cup of coffee in the other hand. "Could we meet after you get off work? Maybe go for a walk or get some dinner?"

Raven's eyes narrowed. "Why?"

"Because I'd like a chance to talk, preferably while I'm not swinging a hammer and you're not torturing my Achilles tendon." He gave her one of his quirky little smiles.

She shook her head. "I can't."

"Why not?" There was a subtle challenge in his eyes as he watched her.

"Because there's a boundary that shouldn't be

crossed, Heath. You drew it there, and now it's my job to keep it in place." *Why won't you understand? I can't handle you walking out on me again.*

Heath hooked one arm around hers and lead her off to the side and away from the coffee shop doors. He set his cup on an empty table nearby. "Leaving Clearwater—leaving you—was the hardest thing I've ever done."

Raven shook her head and moved away from him. He reached out and grabbed her hand before gently tugging her back around to face him.

"I can't understand what all I put you through. But you have to know walking away from us was the biggest mistake of my life."

Heath's eyes begged her to understand. If he'd regretted it, why did he keep his distance? If he truly felt his decision was a mistake, then he should have tried to mend their relationship years ago. Didn't he know she would've gone to Oregon with him in a heartbeat? Raven's stomach ached, and her pulse pounded in her ears. "It's twelve years too late."

This time, when she distanced herself, he didn't try to stop her.

~*~

Saturday afternoon, Heath got out of his truck, prepared to help with the float. He hadn't seen Raven since the other day at the coffee shop. He'd hoped she might show up at the game on Friday. Even Rosie was there, but there was no sign of Raven. When Heath asked her if Raven was feeling okay, Rosie said she was but that her sister wanted to relax for the evening. Heath had no reason to doubt her, but he assumed she was avoiding him. And why shouldn't she?

He'd wasted so much time trying to run away from the guilt. His time at college and then later watching his dreams come true playing for the NFL had been amazing. But through it all, something—someone—had been missing. He'd refused to analyze it too closely then, but now he knew the missing piece of the puzzle was inside that building, and he'd be lucky if she ever spoke to him again.

No matter how long he stood here, nothing was going to change. He finally went inside and spotted Raven at the back of the room near the decorations with a group of three other women. Heath was snatched up by the men who were adding the needed details to the float. The school had voted for a time traveling theme to express how fast four years of high school had flown by. They had to build and mount a large clock along with other details that would be decorated today and next weekend.

Carl and another guy hefted the heavy wooden clock and held it still while Heath nailed it into place. Once the clock was in place, the men stepped back with satisfaction.

"It's coming together," Heath said. He turned to Carl. "How's Rosie feeling this evening?"

"She's good, thanks. She's enjoyed the pregnancy

and said she will be sad to see it end. But I think she's more than ready to get the baby here." He chuckled. "So am I. There's not a lot I can do to help until I can hold Tilly in my arms."

Heath smiled. "Sounds like it won't be too long."

"She's due in about three weeks. Oh! She left specific instructions to invite you to join us Sunday for Rosie and Raven's birthday party."

Heath couldn't be more surprised. Who was inviting him? Seeing as how Raven had avoided him all evening, he doubted it was her. His thoughts must have shown on his face because Carl raised an eyebrow.

"It'll be at their parents' house and the invitation comes from Mrs. Weber." He hesitated. "I know there's a lot of history there. Don't feel obligated to come."

Heath wanted to ask if Raven knew he was invited, but someone called Carl over.

Carl clapped Heath on the shoulder and walked to the front of the room. "Excuse me, everyone." He waited until the garage quieted and all eyes were on him. "We'll be having pizza and drinks available next Saturday at 5 p.m. to thank you all for your time, patience, and skills. We hope you'll be able to make it."

There were cheers as people returned to work.

Heath scanned the room for Raven. She was speaking with someone, her profile to him. He watched as she laughed at something and then pushed her hair behind her ear.

He remembered how soft that hair was when

he'd nearly kissed her last week. There'd been a time when he could've walked across this room and taken her in his arms. Was it a crime to wish he could get that back? To get her back?

He kept hoping he'd have the opportunity to speak with her, but every time he went to get a drink or search her out, she was in the middle of a conversation. By the time five o'clock came around, he'd decided he'd wait around as long as he had to. One way or another, he'd talk to her before he left.

Heath helped clean up and load the extra lumber into a truck. Paint cans they were finished with were separated from those they'd need for touch up next weekend. Most of the volunteers had gone when Heath went inside to find Raven struggling to fold the legs of two long tables. The one she was working on wouldn't budge. Heath crossed the room and reached her as she hit the lever with her palm.

"Here, let me help." Heath tried to flip the lever that held the legs straight and finally had to use the heel of his right shoe to get it to move. "Wow, that was stuck."

"We had enough glue slinging over here tonight, it might have been glued open." Raven offered him a small smile. "Thank you."

"You're welcome." He returned her smile. "I'll get the other table. Where do these go?"

"In that closet over there."

Heath carried each one over to the closet while Raven packed up several boxes. She'd stacked them in a pile and was brushing her hands off on her jeans when he returned. "Is there anything else I can help with?"

"I don't think so. Thank you again."

"You're welcome. Can I walk you out?"

Raven hesitated before finally agreeing. They waved at several people in the parking lot as they walked to Raven's car. Upon reaching it, she immediately unlocked the door and stepped behind it as though it were a shield. "I'm glad things are coming along with the float. I think this may be one of my favorites."

"Mine, too." Heath scratched the back of his neck. "You heading home?"

"Yeah, it's been a long day. Have a good evening, Heath." She got into her car, gave him a wave, and drove off.

Heath frowned as he watched her car disappear. He should've asked if she wanted him to come to her party. Or see if she'd like to join him for dinner. But even as he thought it, he knew she would've turned him down.

How upset would she be if he showed up at her party tomorrow? Uncertainty plagued him as he got in his truck and drove home.

Chapter Twelve

Raven smoothed her black skirt and straightened the teal and black shirt she was wearing. Her mom put one arm around her shoulders and the other around Rosie's. "I can't believe my girls are thirty-one today." She sniffed. "You both look lovely."

Rosie tried to adjust the waist of her dress. "I feel like a whale." She wrinkled her nose and then smiled as she turned to Raven. "It would've been fun if she'd been born on our birthday, wouldn't it? Talk about the best birthday gift ever."

Raven smiled. "Yeah, it would have. But I'm glad she's staying in there to cook a little longer, though."

"Me, too."

The doorbell rang, and Mom leapt into action. "Okay, the celebration has begun!" Hosting parties was one of her favorite things.

Guests arrived over the next half hour. Raven was thrilled that Chrissy made it as well as Mandy,

Preston, and little Barry. Raven hoped they didn't mind that her Mom snatched Barry away and was already making him giggle.

Mandy gave Raven a hug and then handed her a heavy bag. She then put an arm through Preston's and brought him closer. "Go ahead and open it," she said with a smile.

Raven pulled the tissue paper out to find a wooden box inside with the image of a tree of life carved into the top. She carefully lifted it out of the bag, gasping at the details. "Wow, this is gorgeous." She looked at Preston. "Did you make this?"

He nodded and tapped the lid. "It's sized to be a photo box, but you can use it for anything you'd like."

"This is amazing. Thank you both." Raven lifted the lid and admired the construction. Preston's woodworking skill was known through most of Clearwater, and he kept busy shipping handmade and custom items all over the country. She gently set the box on the side table next to her and then hugged her friends.

"How pretty," Chrissy said as she came up behind them. "I should order something for my mom for Christmas." She smiled at Preston and then turned to Raven. "My gift isn't quite so beautiful but..." She whipped a card out and handed it to her.

Raven opened it to find a gift card to her favorite bookstore. "Are you kidding? This is great. Thanks, Chrissy." She hugged her friend.

Preston motioned to the back door. "I'll go see

if your dad needs any help with the grill. Happy birthday, Raven."

"I appreciate it. Thank you so much for coming."

She visited with Mandy and Chrissy another minute or two until the doorbell rang. Raven looked up to find Heath walking into the room, and her breath caught, alerting both friends to the newcomer.

Chrissy looked at Raven in surprise. "Did you invite him?"

"No." She watched as her mom led him right to the snack table. "I'm pretty sure I know who did, though." She sighed. What were her parents thinking?

Heath took the plate Raven's mother handed him and added a cookie to it. His gaze landed on Raven, and he gave her a smile with a hint of uncertainty. Apparently, he wasn't so sure he should be there, either. At least he still had some good sense.

"Are you okay?" Mandy asked.

"Yeah, I'm fine. It's not a big deal, I'm just surprised." She lifted the wooden photo box. "I'll go set this in the guest room so it doesn't get broken. I'll be right back."

Once there, she slipped the gift card inside the box and left it on the dresser. Did she have to go back out there? Maybe she could get away with hiding until it was time to eat. Raven chuckled at herself. Yeah, as if Mom or Dad would ever allow that to happen.

She looked at her reflection in the mirror on the wall above the dresser. "You're thirty-one. It's time to put your big girl panties on." Besides, she'd need to be polite and thank Heath for coming. Hopefully he'd find someone else to visit with for the rest of the evening. Goodness knew half the town were fans of his anyway.

With a deep breath, she raked her fingers through her hair and headed back into the living room. There was no sign of Heath. *Maybe he went out back with most of the other guys.*

Raven found Mom in the kitchen still holding Barry. The moment the little boy caught sight of Raven, he nearly jumped from Mom's arms. Raven laughed as she reached for him and then held him close. "My goodness, you've grown in the last week or two." She patted his back and then made a funny face that had him laughing.

"I think he has, too," Mandy agreed. She smiled at her son and used the neckline of his shirt to swipe at the drool on his chin. "Between the growth spurts and teething, it's been a rough week. He's fooling everyone here, though. Aren't you, buddy? Nobody believes you were up half the night in tears."

"Poor guy." Raven hugged him, but he pushed back again, way too interested in what was going on around him to cuddle for long. When he got squirmy, Mandy took him.

"We may not make it to dessert. If we don't, I'll find you and say goodbye."

Raven nodded. "Mom made a bunch of cupcakes. So if that happens, we'll have plenty for you to take with you." She smiled. "I appreciate you coming. I hope you'll at least get to stay for dinner."

"Me, too. I'm going to take Barry outside for a bit. Happy birthday."

"Thank you." Raven waved at Barry who flapped his hand bye-bye at her. Every time she hugged that baby close, her internal clock kicked into overdrive.

In all truthfulness, she'd expected to be married and have kids by now. In fact, she and Rosie had often talked into the night in high school about their future plans. Raven had hoped to marry early and start a family before she turned twenty-four, while Rosie had hoped to go to college. Funny how, in many ways, their plans had reversed.

She spoke with a neighbor and one of her mom's friends for several minutes. When she turned to see if she could find Chrissy, she discovered Heath walking toward her. "Hey."

"Hey yourself. Happy birthday." He stood with one hand in a pocket and the other behind his back. "Your parents invited me by way of Carl. I hope it's okay that I came."

Raven wanted to tell him it wasn't okay because his presence turned her brain into mush. Every time she saw him, especially in a situation like this where he'd been such a big part of her life before, all their moments together came flooding back.

Instead of speaking her mind, she simply nodded once and said, "Of course."

"Good." Heath pulled his other hand out from behind his back and handed Raven a card. "It's not much, but I didn't want to come empty-handed."

Raven accepted it, her fingertips brushing his in the process. She stared at the red envelope, unsure whether she should open it now or wait.

"You can open it later. There's something smaller inside, and I'd hate for it to fall out and get lost."

Well, at least that answered her question. She held onto the envelope with both hands and gave him a smile. "Thank you. I'll go put it in the guest room with my things." Instead of taking the hint and letting her escape, he moved to follow her.

~*~

Heath didn't know whether he should follow Raven or wait. After this last week, however, this may be the only time he'd have a chance to talk with her alone. She entered the spare room, left the door open, and slid the card he'd given her into a wooden box etched with a very detailed image.

"Wow, that's amazing."

"Isn't it?" Raven ran a hand over the tree. "You remember Mandy, right?"

"I do. I ran into her a few minutes ago." Mandy and Raven had been best friends when he first met Raven. It was nice that they were still close. Of course, that would happen in a small town like Clearwater. An unexpected pang of jealousy went through him as he realized how much of her life he'd missed while so many others had been there for her. He had no right to feel that way, but it was impossible to squelch the emotion.

"Her husband, Preston, made this."

"Now that you say it, I remember hearing about his business. I'll have to look it up." He paused. Raven clasped her hands together. She turned to leave the room when Heath blurted out, "I hate that you're avoiding me, Raven."

She stopped and faced him again, her dark eyes widened with surprise, her attention shifting from him to the door. No one else seemed to notice them. Heath reached out to lightly touch her arm, bringing her gaze back to him. He shifted them to the side where they weren't visible to the rest of the guests and lowered his voice. "I know things have been messed up between us for a long time. I take full responsibility for that. But coming back here and seeing you again…" He took a deep breath to give himself a moment to sort out his thoughts. "Can you look me in the eyes and honestly say you have no feelings for me?"

Raven didn't hesitate. "It doesn't matter."

Heath swallowed his frustration. "Of course it matters." He took a step closer, the toes of his shoes an inch from hers. "I never stopped caring about you. Whether you feel the same way or not matters a great deal to me."

She clasped her hands together in front of her but said nothing. It was clear by the look on her face that she didn't quite believe him.

That she *hadn't* denied having feelings for him bolstered his courage. "What if my injury and return to Clearwater is giving us a second chance? I know things won't be easy, but don't we owe it to ourselves to at least consider the possibility?" He'd messed this up once. Heath had to see if there was still something between them; he couldn't take the regret if he didn't. He'd had more than enough of that to last a lifetime. He said a silent prayer that Raven wouldn't hate him for what he was about to do.

Heath threaded his fingers through her hair at the base of her neck and gently covered her lips with his. She stilled for a heartbeat. Then another. When her lips moved against his, he deepened the kiss. Everything about it—about her—was better than he remembered.

He slipped his other arm around her waist to draw her closer. The sound of her contented sigh made him never want to let her go again.

"Raven?" The sound of Mrs. Weber's voice from outside the door was so unexpected, Heath wasn't sure which of them jumped more.

Raven's hand flew to her mouth, her cheeks bright pink.

Mrs. Weber peeked around the corner, her eyebrows nearly disappearing into her curled bangs. "Dad says dinner will be ready in five minutes." She took in the two of them, the interest on her face less than subtle. "But if you need some time to finish your chat…"

"No." Raven moved to the doorway. "I think

we're good. Thanks, I'm starving." She paused, one hand on the doorframe. When she turned to look at Heath, he couldn't begin to untangle the mix of emotions he saw in her eyes. Raven slipped from the room.

Mrs. Weber gave Heath a sympathetic look that didn't quite mask the hope. Great. Now she'd be on Raven's case, which wouldn't help his own. There was nothing he could do about it now. He followed her out.

A buffet was set up along the counter that extended between the kitchen and the living room. Guests were invited to eat at the kitchen table, in the living room, or to use the patio furniture outside. Personally, Heath intended to go outside for some fresh air.

The food provided at the Weber twins' infamous birthday party was as good as Heath remembered. Mr. Weber could cook a mean burger, and he had a particular seasoning he used on everything that he refused to reveal to anyone. Heath took a large bite and nodded in appreciation. He could pick out the taste of onion, garlic, and even pepper. But there was something else there, too. Did Raven know what it was, or did her father keep it a secret from his own family members?

Carl took a seat in the patio chair next to Heath. He lifted the burger in appreciation. "You can't go wrong with Roy's hamburgers."

"That's the truth." He shouldn't be annoyed that Carl was on a first name basis with Raven's father when

Heath never had been. Then again, it's not like he'd ever gotten to know the man as an adult. Just one more reminder of how much time had passed.

He and Carl chatted about football and coaching for a while as they ate their meal. He never saw Raven come outside.

Everyone finished their food, visited for a half hour, and then Mrs. Weber announced that it was time for cupcakes. She'd arranged them on a three-tier stand making them look fancy. With fresh strawberries, blueberries, or chocolate curls on top of the frosting, there was no doubt there was something for everyone.

Mrs. Weber motioned for Rosie and Raven to stand near the cupcakes in front of everyone. Both sisters did as they were asked and put an arm around each other. The room erupted in a rendition of the birthday song. At the end of it, Raven and Rosie took a bow which earned them laughter and clapping.

Raven smiled at the crowd. "Thank you all so much for being here today. It means a lot to Rosie and me. Turning another year older is more palatable when the experience is shared with friends." Everyone laughed again. Raven looked at Heath for a moment before motioning people forward. "All right, everyone. Come grab yourself a cupcake or two. I think Mom outdid herself this year."

Heath hoped for the opportunity to speak with Raven before the evening ended. Unfortunately, other guests surrounded her, preventing any possibility for a private conversation. When people began to leave,

Heath wished Rosie a happy birthday, thanked her parents for their hospitality, then sought Raven to say goodbye.

He found her visiting with Chrissy and someone else he didn't know. She looked up as he approached.

"I wanted to wish you happy birthday one more time before I head home."

To his surprise, she stood and excused herself. "Let me walk you out." She shot a look at Chrissy that Heath couldn't quite discern before she led him through the house to the front door. They both stepped onto the porch before she closed the door again behind them.

Raven fiddled with her necklace. "It was nice of you to come, Heath. Rosie…" she hesitated, "…and I both appreciate it."

"I'm glad I could help you celebrate." He would've kissed her goodbye except that people were exiting the house regularly, leaving them in a less-than-private location. "Look, Raven—"

"This is too complicated, Heath."

"Last time I was young. Stupid." He reached for her hand and held it in his, softly running his thumb across her palm. "I let us go way too easily. Maybe it's time we tried complicated."

He suppressed a sigh when the front door opened again, and Raven had to turn to say goodbye to another group of guests. It didn't seem like there'd been nearly this many people inside. She glanced at him, gave him a sad smile, and lifted her hand in a wave. Heath returned it and headed for his truck.

As he drove home, he wasn't sure whether this was the start of a new beginning, or if he'd hammered yet another nail into the coffin of his relationship with Raven.

Chapter Thirteen

Rosie and Carl headed home shortly after the last guest left. That meant Raven was now alone with her parents, and if the gleam in her mom's eye was any indication, Raven wished she'd bowed out of the party earlier herself.

Dad pointed to the living room. "I'll go watch TV." He raised an eyebrow at Raven. "Listen to your mother. Come say goodbye before you leave."

Raven groaned. "It's my birthday, Mom. Can we pretend you didn't see what you saw?"

"You're not getting any younger, honey."

Oh, that's what every girl wanted to hear on her birthday. Nice. "I appreciate it. Now that I'm feeling especially good about myself, I'll head home."

Mom chuckled. "All your dad and I want is what's best for you." Her expression grew serious as she placed a hand on Raven's shoulder. "Why are you so against getting back together with Heath? You've always been perfect for each other."

Oh, sure. They were perfect for each other until Heath decided they weren't. Her parents were there, and they saw what it did to her. Why couldn't they get it? "He's leaving again, Mom. As soon as he's out of that boot, he'll be heading back to Cleveland and his real life. What you saw earlier?" Raven waved a hand in the air. "Maybe it was nostalgia. But we don't fit in each other's worlds, and we haven't for a long time." As the words left Raven's mouth, so did the tiny bit of hope that had taken root since their kiss. She hadn't even realized it'd been there until now.

Mom looked sad as she pulled Raven into a hug. "I'm sorry, honey. I don't want to see you giving up so easily."

She called holding a torch for her old fiancé for twelve years giving up too easily? "I'm sorry, too." Raven sighed as she stepped back. She looked around the room. Remnants of the successful birthday party were everywhere. There were more people in attendance than Raven had a chance to visit with. The food was amazing, as usual, and the kindness of all these people she'd known most of her life had left Raven thankful for the community she lived in. "You sure I can't help you clean?"

"I'm sure." Mom smiled as she handed over a container of cupcakes.

"Thank you both for a great birthday and party." She lifted her arm, admiring the silver bracelet's intricately-twisted design. "I love it."

"You're welcome, honey." Mom smiled at her. "We're glad you like it. Make sure you go say goodbye to your dad."

Raven did that and finally made it out the door and to her car. As soon as she buckled the seat belt, she let her head fall back and took a deep breath.

As much fun as the birthday party had been, she'd been too aware of everything Heath did. When he wasn't in the room, she wondered what he was doing. And when they were in the same room together, when she wasn't sneaking glimpses of him, it felt like his eyes were on her. Goosebumps peppered her skin at the memory of what he said and the way he touched her arm.

Raven wanted to open his card but decided to wait until she was home. If she stayed in front of the house too long, her mom or dad would come out to make sure she was okay.

Once she'd entered her living room, she made a point of using the restroom and changing into comfortable pajamas first. She didn't want to look too hurried to open the card. As if someone were spying on her. Raven laughed at herself, made some tea, and curled up on the couch with the gifts. She'd loved everything she received, from the bracelet her parents gave her to the gift card for books.

After looking through them again, she finally lifted the red envelope from where it was lying on the couch beside her. The flap was carefully tucked inside. She opened it and eased the card out. On the cover was a woman leaning against a fence, a cup of coffee in her hands, and the words "Happy Birthday" above. Fitting. The image made her smile.

Inside was a hand-written note.

Raven,

I know I've done a lot to disappoint you. I don't expect you to forget, and I'm not even sure you'll ever be able to fully forgive me. But if you could find it in your heart to let me explain—to tell you what was going on back then—I'd appreciate it.

Happy birthday, Raven. I hope all your dreams come true.
Always,
Heath

P.S. Enjoy the coffee. If you ever need company, let me know.

He wrote his cell phone number at the bottom. Raven opened the smaller envelope to find a gift card to Clearwater Coffee. It was perfect. She ran a finger over the handwriting and smiled. Part of her wanted to call him immediately and find out what he had to say. She couldn't imagine he'd be able to justify to her why he'd never looked back.

What if what he said only confirmed her deepest fears? What if he'd left because she would've held him back? She swallowed hard and pushed conversations she'd intentionally forgotten from invading her mind again.

She wasn't sure she wanted to delve into the past. No telling what that was going to dredge up.

So why did that bothersome smidge of hope keep flaring up in the center of her heart?

Raven reached for her cell phone and stared at the darkened screen. The real question was which would she regret more: giving Heath the chance to explain things, or always wondering what he might have said?

Instead of calling, she added his name to her contacts and then started a text.

"Thanks for coming to the party tonight. The gift card is great." She found a coffee emoji to include with the text before sending it. There. At least she'd thanked him for the gift, which was the polite thing to do.

She tossed her phone on the coffee table, retrieved a cupcake from the container Mom sent, and turned the television on to watch another episode of *Longmire*. Raven barely made it through half of her dessert before her phone pinged.

Raven stared at it several moments before reaching for it and tapping the screen. Heath's name came up along with his response.

"You're welcome. You were right about that place. Best coffee I've ever tasted."

Raven turned her attention back to the episode she was watching, but moments later, another text pinged from Heath.

"Think about what I said. Please. I'd like the chance to explain."

Raven groaned. She never should've sent the text in the first place. She could've thanked Heath briefly for the gift before therapy on Tuesday and called it a day. This was when she needed Chrissy or Mandy here to stage an intervention. They would have kept her from digging a hole big enough to bury herself in.

But it was too late. Heath's text stared at her, demanding a response. She was still holding the phone in her hand several minutes later when it rang, scaring the ever-living snot out of her. The phone went flying, hitting the carpet and sliding under the coffee table where it continued to ring.

Raven smacked her knee on the side of the table as she lowered herself to the floor and retrieved it. Heath's name flashed on the screen. Right before it quit ringing, Raven finally slid her finger across and answered the call. "Hey."

She winced as she sat down again and rubbed her knee. That was going to bruise.

"Hey yourself. You back home, or are you still at your parents' house?"

"I'm home." She almost said something about Mom grilling her but decided against it. "I ate another cupcake I didn't need. Mom sent a dozen of them home with me. I think I'll take them to work tomorrow so I don't eat them all myself."

His deep chuckle made her smile despite herself. There was a moment of silence before he spoke again. "I know you're probably tired and ready to stay in for the night. But if you're up to it, is there any chance we could talk over a cup of coffee?" When she hesitated, he added, "I won't even make you use the gift card. It's on me."

There were many reasons why Raven should say no. But Heath was going to leave again, and when he did, she refused to live with the questions that tormented her before. This time, she wanted to go their separate ways and not look back. She had a feeling listening to what Heath had to say was a big step in that direction.

"Raven?"

"I'm still here. Yeah, sure. Who am I to turn down a free cup of coffee?"

"Awesome." He sounded relieved. "Meet you at Clearwater Coffee in twenty minutes?"

"I'll be there."

The call ended, and Raven turned off the television, the episode she was watching paused at only five minutes in. She regretted the extra cupcake as her stomach fluttered with nerves. "God, help me to listen to what Heath has to say. Help me to move past this and get on with the rest of my life."

~*~

Heath arrived at the coffee shop only ten minutes after he'd spoken with Raven on the phone. He claimed a corner table, hoping it would be easier to talk. A small part of him wouldn't be surprised if she changed her mind. His phone rang, and he was relieved to see it was Benny and not Raven calling to cancel.

"Hey, Benny. What's going on?"

"Not much. I heard you talked to Coach earlier today. Everything okay?"

Heath frowned. "As far as I know. Should I worry?"

"Nah. He was in one of his ticked moods, so I thought I'd ask."

Coach periodically decided the team wasn't doing enough to prepare for the next game. It meant extra work for a few days until he leveled out again. "He's ready for me to get back. I told him I'd let him know as soon as I get this boot off and can be on the field." He glanced at the door and saw Raven approaching through the glass. "I'm sorry to cut you off, but I need to run. I'll call you back in the next day or two."

"Not a problem. Talk to you later."

Heath ended the call. He didn't realize how tense he was until the bell above the door rang and Raven walked inside. She scanned the interior of the shop until her gaze collided with his. A tentative smile played with the corners of her lips as she sat in the chair opposite Heath. "I don't remember the last time I was in here during the evening."

"What? You don't make it in three times a day?" Heath teased. "It's probably a good thing, otherwise that gift card I gave you won't last long."

The sound of her laugh made him smile. He hadn't realized how much he missed it over the years until he'd come back again. He thought about their kiss earlier. There was no doubt she'd kissed him back. There were so many things he wanted to say, but the words wouldn't come. He finally pointed to the menu above the counter. "How about I get us something to drink?"

"I'd better make it a tea. If I drink coffee too late, it'll keep me up."

Heath feigned a look of shock. "You have a coffee limit?"

"Apparently I'm not getting any younger, according to my mom." There was no missing the sarcasm in her voice.

"Was this before or after the birthday party?" He watched her closely, wondering whether her mom had said anything about their kiss.

"After." She blushed.

Heath desperately wanted to know what they spoke about after he'd left. Raven wasn't offering any details, and he wasn't about to ask. "I'm sorry."

Raven shrugged. "I'm used to it. So about getting something to drink…"

She told him what type of tea she liked, and he ordered it along with a vanilla Frappuccino for himself. Once he paid, he sat down again while they waited. They talked about the weather, the float for the parade, and a few other light subjects until their order was ready. They got settled and Heath was trying to decide what to say when Raven spoke first.

"You wanted to tell me something. What is it?"

Raven never was one to mince words. It was something he appreciated about her even back in high school. Goodness knew girls were hard enough to understand as it was. Having a girlfriend—and later a fiancée—who spoke her mind made a lot of things easier.

Heath gave a half laugh and ran a hand across the back of his neck. "I'm not sure where to begin."

"How did you consider breaking things off between us before you actually did?"

Okay, maybe a little less outspoken wouldn't be a bad thing. He watched as Raven cupped her hands around her tea, her eyes on the steam as it dissipated into the air.

Heath took a drink before answering. "Honestly? It was a week. Maybe two. It wasn't like I'd made this big decision and then couldn't tell you. I don't know..." He sighed. "I was selfish, Raven. About a lot of things. I got that scholarship, and it didn't matter what happened, I was going there to play football and get a degree in business." He gave her a sad smile. "And you were willing to give up everything here to go with me. I took that for granted. I didn't even consider what you might be leaving behind."

Raven blinked at him. "We'd talked about our future. Our plans. That's what we both wanted. We could go to school there, get married, come back to visit our families."

"Where would we end up living, Raven?" When she gave him a blank stare, he continued. "That week leading up to high school graduation, when you were so busy shopping for dresses with your sister and mom, I worried about whether you would be happy moving away from everything you knew. It was something Pop warned me about over and over again."

Now Raven looked shocked. "He what?"

"He told me you and I were too different. That you were someone who'd regret leaving her hometown, and I was destined to go and never look back. He said you'd wake up one day and blame me for ruining your life." That conversation had haunted him, and he could hear it replaying in his head as if it were yesterday. "I didn't want to believe him."

She fingered the paper sleeve on her cup a moment before looking up at him. "I knew it would be hard to leave Clearwater, Heath. But I'd planned on it for you. For us." She picked up the cup as if to get a drink but set it back down again. "Your decision to break our engagement felt like it came from so far out in left field, it didn't seem real. Not at first. I kept expecting you to change your mind or want to talk about it. Something." Raven brought her bottom lip in between her teeth, emotions dancing in her eyes. "You said you didn't want to believe your father. What was it that tipped the scale? Was it something I did or didn't say? If I ever gave you any impression you weren't enough for me back then…"

"No." Heath reached across the table and covered one of her hands with his. "That wasn't it at all. My father overheard you and Rosie talking at one of the football games. You told her you were giving up one family for another. She asked you if you were coming home for Christmas and you said you didn't know. That it would depend on me. Pop said you were in tears." Raven started to shake her head, but Heath stopped her. If he didn't get this all out now, he might not ever tell her what happened. He cringed. "Pop gave up playing football because of his heart, but he moved here to Clearwater for Mom. I grew up hearing about his regrets. There were times I wondered if he regretted getting married. Or having me." He shook his head and squeezed her hand. "In that moment, all I could think of was you. I couldn't handle it if you regretted leaving your life behind to follow me to who knows how many towns. Raven, I moved six times in the first five years after I graduated college. That wasn't the kind of life I wanted for you."

He turned her hand over in his and traced the lines of her palm with his thumb. "If you ever resented me the way my father—" He swallowed. "Back then, I broke our engagement for you. At least, that's what I told myself."

Raven's back stiffened, and she pulled her hand away. "That wasn't fair, Heath. You never should have made that kind of decision without even talking to me." She leaned against the back of her chair, her arms crossed in front of her. "I knew what I was getting into. I knew it wouldn't be easy. But we would've figured it out together." Her voice broke. "I have no idea what conversation your father overheard. I said nothing like that to Rosie."

"You love everything about this town. This is where you've always belonged. To ask you to give it up—to leave your family behind…"

"Don't you get it? You were supposed to be my family."

The sadness in her eyes stole the breath from his lungs. She was right about so many things. "I get that now. But back then, I let my fears dictate everything else. It wasn't right, Raven. But that's the truth." He stared at his Frappuccino which had remained untouched and was now mostly melted. When his gaze lifted to collide with hers, he saw a myriad of questions in her eyes. "I never stopped loving you. I can't tell you how many times I'd wished I'd called you. Or come back and spoken to you about my fears. I wondered for years how different our lives would've been."

"Why didn't you?" Her question was barely above a whisper.

"I figured you hated me. The longer I stayed away, the more difficult it was to reconnect with you. And after a while, I figured you'd moved on." He'd been so stupid. "I hated myself for what I did to you. To us."

"I waited, Heath. For months, I waited, hoping you'd change your mind and come back. I watched for your phone calls and imagined you walking back into town. I tried to move on after a while, believe me." Her eyes filled with tears, and it was unclear whether they were caused by sadness, anger, or a mix of the two.

"But no matter what I did or how hard I tried, I never stopped loving you, either." She swiped at a single tear that escaped and slid down her cheek.

What was Heath supposed to say to that? Any other time, if Raven admitted she still loved him, he would've gathered her in his arms and kissed her until they were both breathless. But this was different. Right now, she looked as uncertain as he felt. "Where do we go from here, Raven?"

Her brown eyes studied him. "I wish I knew."

Chapter Fourteen

Raven's eyes fluttered open, and she flinched against the bright morning sun. Everything about her conversation with Heath at the coffee shop last night came flooding back. She groaned. They'd talked until the place closed and then went their separate ways. They both agreed they needed space and time to think. Raven had done a lot of thinking, praying, and crying until after two this morning when she finally fell asleep.

Now it was six-thirty in the morning, and she needed to get ready for work. The lack of sleep, and the exhaustion from crying once she'd gotten home, made her wish she could take the day off and go back to bed.

Raven might have done that except she'd be seeing April today at CRC. She dragged herself out of bed, showered, and drove back to Clearwater Coffee. The moment she stepped up to the counter to place her order with Chrissy, Raven's friend frowned. "Wow, you look tired. You okay?"

"Oh, sure." She didn't even try to sound convincing. "There's not enough caffeine in this place to get me through today."

"This is serious." She took her ten-minute break and practically dragged Raven to a corner table. "Spill."

"Girl, if I do, I'll end up bawling again, and that's the last thing I need before work." Raven sighed. "We talked. He told me he never stopped loving me and regretted leaving back then." She paused. "I may have told him I never stopped loving him either."

Chrissy's eyes widened. "Are you two getting back together again? Talk about an epic love story!"

Raven glanced around the coffee shop, hoping she didn't see anyone she recognized. "No! At least, I don't think so. He's leaving again, Chrissy. I can't go through that a second time. So where does that leave us?"

Chrissy's smile faded into a sad frown. "I don't know, Raven. But if you two are meant for each other, something will work out."

"Yeah. I wish God would clue me in on the plan. A nudge. A whisper. Something." Raven lifted her hands and shrugged her shoulders. "Heath seemed sincere, but what if he isn't? I'm not even sure we know each other anymore."

"I doubt the guy has kept a candle burning for you for twelve years only to string you along now." Chrissy gave her friend a firm look. "Maybe you two were always meant to be. Just not twelve years ago.

What if things had to change in both of you? Maybe things are finally where they need to be so you can be together."

"I'm not sure I can work with 'ifs' and 'maybes,' Chrissy. Seriously, what am I supposed to do?" Raven had always preferred to face a problem head-on and fix it. This waiting around business was for the birds. How could she gamble with the future at a risk of repeating the past? It was a lot to ask of anyone. She finally shrugged and then collapsed against the back of her chair. "We may have been born in the same town, but it feels like we're worlds away from each other now."

"Then pray. Pray that God will help separate the fears and second-guessing from the equation, so you can see the answer. Then pray He will give you peace no matter what that answer is." Someone called for Chrissy, and she nodded holding up a single finger to tell him she'd be there in a moment.

"You make it sound so easy."

"Oh, it's not easy at all. But it's better than trying to handle it yourself." She reached over and patted Raven on the arm. "Come on, let's get you that coffee before you fall asleep."

Raven leaned over the table, rested her forehead on her arm, and let loose with a loud, fake snore. When she looked up again, she managed a smile. "Thanks, Chrissy. I appreciate it, I hope you know that."

"You'd better." Chrissy pasted a smug look on her face that lasted three seconds before she busted out laughing. "Everything will work out. Call me if you need to chat, okay?"

"I will." Raven waited for her coffee and then left with a wave.

She got into her car and then sat there for a few minutes before starting the engine. "All right, God. Obviously, I have no idea what I'm doing down here. And since You don't seem too keen on sending road maps my way, how about You take the wheel for a while?" It seemed so cliché, yet the moment the words left her mouth, the weight on Raven's shoulders felt a little bit lighter.

~*~

Heath made it through Monday without calling or texting Raven, but it'd taken a great deal of effort. By the time he arrived at CRC for his therapy session, he was going stir-crazy. When he and Raven parted ways at the coffee shop, he had no idea what she was thinking. The moment she'd told him she'd never stopped loving him either, his hope soared. Maybe there was a second chance hiding in the shadows. But the longer they went without talking, the more the doubts settled again.

With no one to talk to, he'd had to hash it all out on his own. Unfortunately, that hadn't gotten him any closer to solving their problem.

He sat in the room, his eyes on the closed door in front of him. He could be frustrated with Raven and her lack of contact all he wanted, but it was ultimately his fault. It was his choice to end their engagement in the first place and then never call her again.

There were two things he did know: he'd shot himself in the foot when he walked away from Raven, and he was still in love with her. He wanted her in his life. Heath hoped he hadn't waited too long.

There was noise outside as a shadow blocked the light at the bottom of the door. After a moment, there was a light knock as it opened. Raven stepped through, wearing a pair of bright purple scrubs. She closed the door behind her and offered him a small smile. "How's your day going?"

"It's getting better." Heath couldn't hold back a grin of his own. Way to keep it cool. "How about you?"

"I started the day off with a coffee someone else bought me, so I can't complain."

He chuckled. "Well, I hope the guy at least bought you the good stuff."

"Eh, it was okay." She tossed him a saucy smile before replacing it with a more serious expression. "Seriously, though, thanks again for the gift card."

"You're welcome."

They began the therapy session like normal. As Heath worked through the isometric exercises, there was very little discomfort. He told Raven as much.

"That's a great sign. I wouldn't be surprised if Dr. Bright wants you out of that boot next week."

Raven's voice sounded normal, but Heath saw conflicting emotions before she schooled her features. He didn't have to ask her what she was thinking, though. Once he had the boot off, it meant it'd be easier for him to transfer back to the team physician in Cleveland. They stared at each other for a heartbeat or two before he re-focused on his exercises. It was horrible, but for the first time since he'd injured himself, he wished his recovery wasn't going forward quite so quickly.

Or maybe he wished they'd spoken earlier. It would have given them more time to work through everything.

"Do you want to get pizza and shoot pool with me Friday night?" He watched as she looked at him in surprise.

The corners of her mouth lifted. "Pool, huh? I haven't played in so long…"

A local church had a family center with pool tables, table tennis, a gym for basketball, and a roller skating rink. Every Friday night, they made it available to the public, encouraging families to do something together and give kids a safe place to hang out. Heath lost count of how many times he and Raven had met there and hung out with friends. They'd both gotten quite good at pool back in the day.

"I haven't either. You'll probably beat me. You always were the pool shark."

She laughed outright at that. Truthfully, he's the one who'd won nearly every time. But she was always a good sport and they had fun. Especially when she'd come up with outrageous handicaps to even up the playing field.

He raised an eyebrow at her. "Is that a yes?"

Raven unconsciously ran a finger over the scar near her mouth and finally gave a small nod. "Okay."

There was no holding back his grin. "If you'll text me your address, I'll even come by and pick you up like a gentleman. Does six sound okay?"

"That'll be fine." She glanced at her watch. "But we'd better get moving in here, or I'll have to cut the session off. I've got another patient in ten minutes."

"Yes, ma'am." His exaggerated drawl coaxed another smile from her. He didn't dare try to kiss her here, but Friday night was a whole different matter.

~*~

"I still can't believe Jerome's Pizza is out of business."

Raven laughed as they left a more well-known pizza restaurant. They'd enjoyed splitting a pepperoni pizza and breadsticks. But Heath couldn't let go of the fact that his favorite pizza place had closed down nearly ten years ago. "A lot has changed around here. You'd be surprised." It wasn't meant as a dig at how long he'd been gone, but she realized it might have sounded that way as soon as the words left her lips. Heath opened the passenger door for her, and she got settled inside. "Sorry, I didn't mean that the way it sounded."

"No, it's okay." Heath shrugged as he stood in the door. "It seems like every other day I've been back,

I discover another way that life here has changed. I can't expect things to be any different." There was a hint of wistfulness in his tone. "I try to remind myself most of them would've changed whether I was here or not."

"That's true. Most of them probably would have." She smiled to try and lighten the mood. "Although you ate at Jerome's often enough, it may have been the lack of your business that put the place under."

"Ha, ha, very funny." He shook his head at her. "I'm glad you agreed to go out with me tonight."

"Me, too." Raven was on a date with Heath. The whole thing was a bit surreal. That they were ever engaged seemed like an entire lifetime ago. Yet, as she stared into his eyes, it also felt like yesterday.

Heath hesitated then laughed at himself. "You know what? I'm going to close this door and drive us over to the family center." He raised his eyebrows, did as he said, and got behind the wheel.

When they arrived, the parking lot was busy. Heath found a spot and went around to open the door for Raven. "Wow, this place has changed, too."

Raven got out and they walked side by side to the entrance. "They closed it down for several months two years ago and completely renovated the place. I haven't been in since they did all that. Someone said they put in a bowling alley."

"No way. I'm glad to see this place is still ministering to families like this." Heath paid the small fee that allowed them access to the activities and games inside. Once through the door, the sounds of children laughing, pool balls hitting each other and rolling across the tables, and video game machines filled the air.

A wave of nostalgia swept through Raven. Memories surfaced. They'd spent a lot of time here having fun, hanging out together, and laughing, even before they'd started dating. A couple walked by, their young son between them, and Raven swallowed hard. Maybe coming here wasn't the best idea.

Heath must have sensed her mood. Or maybe all the memories were haunting him, too. Either way, he reached for her hand, laced their fingers together, and led the way to the pool tables. They played two games and quickly discovered playing pool was not at all like riding a bike.

Raven laughed so hard she doubled over, her palms on the edge of the table. "That was horrible," she said, ending with a snort that had her laughing more. When she lifted her head, she found Heath watching her, a huge grin on his face as he shook his head.

"It wasn't that bad."

"Oh, but it was." She put chalk on the end of her pool stick. "I almost hit that poor kid over there. They're going to ban me from ever coming back after this."

Heath leaned his pool stick against the table and moved to stand next to her. "You need to hold the stick differently. Here, let me show you."

Raven's breath rushed from her lungs as he put his arms around her and helped her adjust the way she was aiming. "Okay, now try it."

His breath tickled the hair near her ear. How was she supposed to concentrate on anything when he was standing so close? His arm brushed against hers, and she desperately tried to focus enough to keep from making a complete fool of herself.

She didn't sink the ball she was aiming for, but at least no one was hurt in the process. She straightened and shrugged.

Heath chuckled. "Then again, it's not like I'm playing any better. What do I know?"

Raven laughed then. "We're quite a pair, huh?"

Only after she spoke did she realize what she'd said. Heath's gaze settled on hers for several breaths before he moved to take his turn.

They finished the game and sat down in chairs near the snack area. Raven placed one foot on the edge of her chair and rested her arm against it as she watched the surrounding people. There was one group of high school-aged kids laughing and carrying on by the arcade games. "It's hard to believe we were ever that age, isn't it?"

"Yeah, it sure is." He smiled. "I still remember the first time I met you. It was the first day of English, and you told me I was full of myself. Do you remember that?"

Raven's cheeks warmed. Heath had been so

determined that his view of the play their teacher read aloud was correct that he hadn't been willing to listen to any other opinions. "Well, you were." She lifted an eyebrow at him.

"You didn't like me at first, did you?"

She hadn't. In fact, she'd told Mandy that if she ever had to speak to Heath again, it would be too soon. "I guess you grew on me after a while."

"How about now?"

Raven turned her head to find Heath watching her, his expression serious. "What do you mean?"

"I wouldn't blame you if you hated me after I left."

She sighed and fiddled with the ends of her hair. "I don't think I ever hated you, Heath. I was disappointed. Hurt. Confused. I blamed you, blamed myself." She met his eyes. "I don't think I've ever been as angry with anyone as I was with you. If you'd asked me that question six months or a year later, I might have said yes, but not now."

Heath flinched but, to his credit, said nothing as he listened.

Raven gave a little shrug. "I finally decided that I couldn't live in the past. That I had to move forward with my life. That's when I enrolled in San Antonio. I had to let you go like you had me. But it was one of the hardest things I've ever done." Tears built up, and she tried desperately to blink them away. "It wasn't easy. You were my first love, Heath. And you'd broken my heart."

He took her hand in his and placed a light kiss to the back of it. "I'm so sorry, Raven. For everything I put you through. For taking that life we'd planned together and throwing it away." He offered her a tired smile. "I guess I should thank you for not hitting me or running me over or something when I got back to town."

That got a chuckle out of her. "Are you kidding? I've been getting some of my revenge through therapy." She gave him a wink that had him smiling.

They sat for a while and talked about the memories they both shared from their high school days.

When the family center announced they were closing in ten minutes, Heath and Raven stood together to leave. "I guess I should take you home," he said as he held the door open for her. They walked across the parking lot, lit up with bright lights overhead. Once they were settled in the truck, he started the engine and drove her back to her place, then walked her to her door. It was a good thing she'd left the porch light on, although the number of moths flittering around it made them both duck more than once. "I assume you'll be there to work on the float tomorrow?"

Oh, tomorrow was Saturday. "Of course. It's the last volunteer day, I can't ruin my perfect attendance record now." She thought about the party afterward and patted her middle. "Though if I'd remembered the pizza party, I might have suggested we eat somewhere else tonight."

"Nah, there's no such thing as too much pizza."

The sparkle in his eyes made her laugh. "Maybe so. Though my mom disagrees. She likes to remind me I'm not a spring chicken and should watch what I eat."

Heath shook his head. "She has no idea what she's talking about. You look more beautiful now than you did when we were in high school."

His words caused her heart to tumble around in her chest. He'd always said the sweetest things back then. It would seem his ability to have the right words at the right time hadn't changed. If he kept on like this, it would make it all the harder to keep an emotional distance. "Heath…"

Before she could say another word, he'd closed the distance between them and gently cradled her face with his hands. His lips touched hers in a kiss so sweet and gentle, she thought she might melt into a puddle at their feet. Way too soon, he leaned back again and smiled. "Good night, Raven."

Raven stood at the doorway, a finger resting on her lips, as she watched him walk back to his truck. He gave her a small wave and then drove away.

Every moment with Heath only reawakened the love she'd tried to keep buried. What was she going to do when he left again and took her heart along with him?

Chapter Fifteen

"What's with the goofy grin?" Chrissy set the container of coffees on the table nearby and fixed Raven with a knowing look.

"I have no idea what you're talking about." Raven made a point of not looking across the garage where Heath was working on the float.

"Uh-huh. And the suspicious grin that appears every time a certain running back walks by has nothing to do with it."

Raven grimaced. And here she thought she'd been keeping it cool. The last thing she needed was for rumors to fly around and get back to her parents. She hadn't worked through her own mess of emotions; she certainly didn't need her parents' input.

She waited until a couple of people moved away and then lowered her voice. "I'm a glutton for punishment. I'm letting him get to me again, letting myself hope for something that'll never work."

"Why not?" Chrissy leaned against the edge of one table and quirked an eyebrow at her friend. "Seriously, even I can tell there's something between you two. Something special. I think it's worth fighting for."

"He'll leave again. I can't fight for something that isn't here." Raven sighed. She noticed a guy pass by who didn't try to hide his interest in Chrissy. "I think you've got an admirer."

Chrissy followed Raven's gaze and immediately shook her head. "Uh, no." Her cheeks darkened.

"Why not?"

"Because I went out with him a few weeks ago. Then one day he came into the coffee shop with another date." She wrapped the blue section of her hair around one finger.

"Wow. What a jerk." Raven gave her friend a hug. "Come on, we need to stop talking about our non-existent love lives and get to work." She observed the progress with satisfaction. "One thing you can't fault Clearwater High for: commitment."

"That's the truth."

The large group of volunteers finished with the list of projects early and began to clean up while Carl and a couple other guys went to pick up the pizza and sodas.

The food barely made it to the tables before people swarmed in to grab slices and visit as they ate.

Raven took her plate and sat on the curb outside where it wasn't as crowded. She hadn't been there more than a minute before she heard footsteps behind her.

"Is this seat taken?" Heath didn't wait for her response before sitting beside her. He tilted his head toward her plate. "You're being a rebel tonight, I see."

She chuckled. "If choosing sausage over pepperoni is being a rebel, I am in desperate need of excitement in my life." She took a bite and had to use the other hand to gather up the string of cheese that followed. "It's good."

Heath took a bite twice the size of what she had. "It sure is."

They ate as they talked about the float and the parade, game, and homecoming the following weekend.

When they finished their pizza, Heath reached over and took her plate, putting it on top of his. "I'll be right back."

He must have thrown them away because he returned empty handed. He rejoined her on the curb. "You know, someone talked me into attending the game and going to the homecoming dance as a chaperone. I might not stick out like a sore thumb so much if I weren't going alone." He gave her one of his flirty grins. "Would you do me the honor of going to homecoming with me, Raven?"

That was not a good idea. Raven's brain warred with her heart, and before she'd reached a resolution, her mouth answered for her. "Since a certain sister of mine talked me into filling in for her as well, it'd be a shame to not go together."

Heath raised an eyebrow at her. "That wasn't quite the resounding yes I'd hoped for, but I'll take it." He leaned over and bumped her shoulder with his. "I'd like to take you to lunch. Maybe go to the parade together and make a day of it. Do you work that afternoon?"

The schools all had a half day next Friday, and CRC did the same. A lot of businesses closed early so people could attend the community event. "No, I don't have to work." She usually avoided the parade and the smothering crowds. It was bad enough that she had to attend the game and the dance that night, too. Then again, if she went to the parade with Heath, maybe it wouldn't be as bad.

"Good. I'll pick you up at twelve-thirty." He leaned over then and placed a light kiss to her cheek. "With any luck, maybe I'll get rid of this boot by then and convince you to dance with me."

His mention of the boot dampened Raven's spirits, and she tried not to think about what that ultimately meant. She forced herself to smile. "Don't count on it, cowboy."

~*~

Heath was happy to see Dr. Bright come in with Raven the following Tuesday at CRC. By the end of the session, he'd ditched the boot completely. When Dr. Bright informed him he could keep it, Heath politely declined. He was more than happy to leave it behind.

Dr. Bright did most of the talking as she went over what the rest of his physical therapy would look like for the following months. "We thank you for choosing CRC. Know you're welcome to stay here as long as you'd like. I will send a report over to your team doctor today as well, though, so you can transfer back at your convenience."

Heath glanced at Raven, but she remained stoic. "I appreciate it, thank you." He flexed his foot. "It may take a while to get back to normal, but getting rid of that blasted thing will make all the difference."

By the time Dr. Bright left, the session was nearly over. They worked on a few of the isometrics, but Raven wasn't her normal talkative self. Heath didn't want to press her, either. Before she opened the door, and he headed to the gym, he put an arm around her shoulders. "Are we still on for Friday?" She nodded. "Good. I'll text or call later, okay?"

"Okay."

He wished he knew what to say to make that frown on her pretty face disappear. But he didn't have the words.

They only talked for a few minutes that night and texted a time or two on Wednesday. It was bothering him that he couldn't go see her in person, but he sensed she needed some space. Thursday night, he headed over to his parents' house for dinner. Mom had cooked a roast and insisted he come and share it.

Heath had forgotten how much he enjoyed his mom's roast. He slathered it and the mashed potatoes with brown gravy. "This looks amazing. Thank you again."

"You're welcome." She grinned as she watched him dig into his meal. "Your father and I are looking forward to the game tomorrow."

Heath smiled and nodded. Once he'd swallowed his mouthful, he replied, "I am, too. Carl asked me to join the team on the sidelines, so that should be fun." He said nothing about spending the afternoon with Raven or taking her to the dance. Heath wasn't in the mood to deal with the negative response that would have followed. His mom made this big meal, and Heath didn't want it ruined by his father's inability to hold his tongue.

They'd finished eating when Heath's phone rang. Surprised, he took it out of his pocket and swiped the screen to answer it. "Hello. This is Heath."

"Hey there, Shaw."

There was no missing that commanding voice, even if this was the last person he'd expected to hear from tonight. "Hey, Coach." He noticed Pop sitting up straighter in his seat, his eyes focused on his son.

"Dr. Drover said you got the all clear to get back to work and start training again. We pushed the transfer through with your insurance. Any chance you could get back to town Monday?"

This was all he'd wanted when he first came back to Clearwater. At that time, being away from the team made him feel disconnected. But now... Now the thought of leaving again gave him an unsettled feeling in the pit of his stomach. This was his job, though. And that look his father was giving him was a reminder of exactly that. A thousand thoughts swirled in his head as the sound of his pulse echoed in his ears. "I'm sure I can arrange that. Yes, sir. I'll see you then." He hung up and slipped the phone back into his pocket.

Pop clapped his hands and rubbed them together. "Aha! I knew they'd welcome you back with open arms. Training on the field on top of physical therapy there will get you where you need to be in no time."

Mom's reaction was nearly the opposite. She seemed happy for Heath, but there was a sadness in her eyes as well. No matter what happened, he'd make a point of coming back for Christmas. Too much time had already passed; he wasn't going to let that happen again.

His father was still talking about Heath's return to Cleveland. "I bet you'll be out on the field during games before the end of the season."

Heath had started out with that same level of enthusiasm, but now he wasn't so sure. He wasn't sure of anything. "I hope so, Pop. But I'm going into this realistically. You know only two thirds of players with a ruptured Achilles go back, and those that do rarely play on the same level as they did before."

"It's all attitude. If you put the work in, you'll be fine. Keep your head in the game, Heath. What happens is up to you."

Heath suppressed a wave of sadness as Mom stood, patted him on the shoulder, and said, "I'll take these dishes into the kitchen and get dessert ready." She didn't want to hear any more about it, and Heath didn't blame her.

He considered saying nothing, but after she left, he couldn't help himself. "Would it be so bad if I retired early, Pop?"

"You'll do no such thing. What's wrong with you? Are you willing to take your entire career and flush it down the toilet?" He threw the napkin he was holding onto the table as if he were throwing a ball to the ground for a touchdown. "I will not allow you to make that mistake. There's no reason why you can't get back on that field if you put your mind to it." His father was so angry that his face had turned red as his hands clenched.

"It's been a dream come true to play for the NFL. But I've always known it wouldn't be forever. It never is. I've saved my money, invested in several businesses here in Clearwater, and I've set myself up a fund for retirement."

His father shook his head as though at a loss for words. "If you do that, you'll never be happy. You'll regret that decision for the rest of your life." He stood and left the room. A moment later, the front door opened and closed again.

Heath placed his palms on the edge of the table. He ought to be angry at Pop, but all he felt was sorry for him. Mom came back in then with two plates, a piece of chocolate cake on each of them. Wordlessly, she handed one to Heath and sat down with the other.

"I'm sorry, Mom."

"This is all your father." She frowned as she lifted a bite of cake and chewed thoughtfully. "He spends so much time looking backward, he misses everything he's going through now. One day he will realize that. I hope it won't be too late."

The sadness on her face pulled at Heath's heartstrings. "You're a saint, Mom. I hope Pop sees that one day, too." He lifted a forkful of cake. "Not to mention you make the best cake in Clearwater. I appreciate dinner, it was great."

"You're welcome." She reached under the table and tapped his foot with her own. "So you going back on Monday?"

"Yeah, probably so. But coming back for Christmas, Mom. I promise."

She smiled then, tears in her eyes. "I'll hold you to that."

There were a million things he needed to accomplish over the next couple of days. None of them occupied his thoughts like the worry of how he was going to tell Raven.

Chapter Sixteen

Raven checked the weather first thing Friday morning. There had been a small chance of rain the night before, but thankfully that had disappeared. With the parade taking place at one in the afternoon, rain would've put a huge damper on the festivities. Raven only remembered the parade being canceled once or twice in the last decade. While she hadn't intended to go anyway, many members of the community had been disappointed. After the amount of work they'd put into the float, she could understand that more now.

She finished work at noon and hurried home to change. She ditched her scrubs for a pair of jeans and a long-sleeved dark green blouse. With the walking she knew they'd do at the parade and later the game, she chose to wear her tennis shoes.

Heath arrived at her house at exactly twelve-thirty. She answered the door with a smile. "You're right on time."

"I try." He grinned. "You ready to go? I figured we could pick up something for lunch at one of the food trucks on the square and eat while we watch the parade."

"That sounds great." Raven locked the door behind her and glanced up at the sky. Even the clouds were clearing, giving way to blue sky and sunshine. "I'm anxious to see how that float looks going down Main Street. Hopefully it stays together. Goodness knows we used enough glue." They got into his truck. "I'm surprised the team didn't ask you to join them on the float."

"They did, but I told them I had other plans." He gave her a wink as he pulled away from the curb.

He'd chosen to spend time with her instead of waving to his adoring fans. The realization warmed her. "I'm glad."

"They asked me to sit on the sidelines with them at the game, though. I didn't feel like I could turn them down twice. I hope that's okay." He glanced at her as though nervous about her response.

"That's fine. I wouldn't dream of keeping Clearwater's own football star in the stands during the homecoming game."

He reached for her hand and kissed her wrist before releasing it again. "You're pretty amazing, you know that?"

She shrugged, not sure what to say. She smiled to herself as they maneuvered through the crowded streets and finally found a parking spot several blocks away from the town square. As they strolled down the sidewalk, Heath again reached for her hand. This time he laced their fingers together, seemingly in no hurry to let go again. Neither was Raven. She enjoyed the physical connection as they browsed the food trucks and decided on chicken street tacos.

With their plates of food in hand, they found a spot on Main Street near where the parade was supposed to begin and ate while they waited.

Music started up long before the parade turned the corner and came into view. The crowd cheered as the mayor and his family drove by in an antique car, waving. Behind them, a variety of businesses with colorful floats and fun music strolled down the street.

People on the floats cheered and threw candy as they went, which was a highlight for the kids in the crowd. They swarmed the curbs to pick up the bright orbs of sugar and add them to the bags they'd brought.

The local 4H group came through on a variety of beautiful horses. Raven leaned closer to Heath. "I wish I'd learned how to ride."

He turned toward her, inches away, surprise on his face. "You? On a horse?"

Raven planted a hand on her hip. "Yes. What's so weird about that?"

His lips lifted in a grin. "I'm sorry, I can't picture it." Then he chuckled. "Okay, yes, I can."

"Hey!" She used her shoulder to hit his and was surprised by how much solid muscle she encountered.

She rubbed her arm. "Ouch." That only had him laughing harder. She couldn't keep a straight face and soon was covering her own smile with a palm. "Okay, fine. Maybe becoming a world-known horseback rider is not in my future."

"Yeah, I'm not thinking it is."

"Thanks for that." She wasn't the least bit offended, though. Especially when he put an arm around her waist and tugged her close as they continued to watch the parade.

At one point, someone tossed out wrapped pieces of chocolate. Heath stooped and retrieved one, handing it to Raven with a smile and a flourish. She unwrapped it and popped it into her mouth, thinking it may be one of the sweetest pieces of chocolate she'd ever had.

She caught sight of the clock at the top of their float as it rounded the corner. "Oh, here it comes!" Raven bounced on her toes to get a better look. She had to admit it looked pretty good out there.

The football team stood on the float in their uniforms while the cheerleaders led the way with flips and twirls to engage the crowd. Behind the float, the high school band played as they kept in perfect step together.

Raven scanned the surrounding people, recognizing more than a handful of them. Mrs. Giles from the corner market caught her eye and waved with a smile. Raven waved back. This was what she loved about Clearwater and living in a town her whole life.

You couldn't find this kind of community spirit just anywhere.

What did Heath think about all of this? Had he missed it? Or was he content in the moment, but would be as happy to go back to Cleveland again? Her runaway train of thought was putting a serious damper on her spirits.

Whether Heath sensed her change in mood, or the timing was right, Raven didn't know. He put a hand on each of her shoulders and massaged them gently before leaning her back against his chest. With his arms around her waist, he rested his cheek against hers, and they finished watching the rest of the parade.

Being held by Heath didn't fix their situation, and Cleveland didn't magically disappear. Still, it made Raven daydream that they could somehow make things work. She was probably fooling herself, but it was a lot better than reality.

The moment the last vehicle ended, the crowd began to disperse. Those going to the football game afterward would head that way shortly. Everyone else was hoping to get to their cars and home again before too much traffic clogged the downtown roads.

"I guess we should get going." Heath's soft words were spoken next to Raven's ear and sent electricity dancing down her spine.

"I guess we should."

Neither of them moved for several moments. The crowd of people pushing past them got them moving. They walked hand in hand back to Heath's truck. Their slow progress through traffic led them to the large parking lot outside of the busy high school football stadium.

They took their time walking along the path that led around the stadium. Heath squeezed her hand. "I wish I hadn't agreed to sit on the field with the team now."

Yeah, so did she. But the boys were counting on Heath to be there. Besides, they were going to the dance together later, so she pushed her disappointment aside. "It's okay. I'll find you when the game's over."

Heath glanced over his shoulder. With a mischievous grin on his face, he tugged her hand and led her off the path to a tree not far away. Once they'd skirted the large trunk and paused on the other side, Heath turned to face her. With one hand on the bark behind her shoulder, he leaned close. "It'll be a while before I see you again. I may go through withdrawals. Any idea what might help with that?"

Raven shook her head, a smile on her face. "You're so full of it, you know that?"

"You objecting?"

"No." Her voice sounded breathless and then Heath was kissing her. She placed her hand flat against his chest as he deepened the kiss. The moment didn't last nearly long enough. Her cheeks burned when he broke their connection and gave her a smile that made her pulse race.

Like a gentleman, he led her to the stands and didn't leave again until she was settled. She watched him go back down the steps to disappear in the crowd. Only then did she allow herself to sag against her seat and process the emotions racing through her.

Everything about the day had been perfect from the street tacos, to the parade, to that amazing kiss they'd just shared. It felt right, as if they'd somehow picked up where they left off years ago. It was amazing and scary all at the same time.

Raven was more in love with Heath now than she ever was before. Where did that leave them?

Several people Raven knew stopped to say hi, bringing with them a welcome break from her rambling thoughts. She visited with them for a while until they moved to their seats, making way for someone else she recognized.

Raven visited with people as much as she watched the game for the first hour. When she found herself alone again, she decided a snack was in order before halftime when the concession stand would become flooded. She picked her way through the crowd. She was feet away from the end of the line when Heath's father stopped her.

"Oh! Hi, Mr. Shaw. Are you enjoying the game?"

"I am." Mr. Shaw nodded, his gaze moving past her and resting on the field beyond. "It was great for the team to invite Heath down to sit with them."

"Yes, it was." There was something about the way Mr. Shaw avoided eye contact that put Raven on alert. She motioned toward the line that was moving forward without her. "Were you on your way to get a snack?"

"Actually, I was hoping to chat with you a moment." He motioned toward an area off to the side where it wasn't as crowded. He waited for Raven to precede him.

Once there, Mr. Shaw studied her with a frown that accentuated the lines next to his mouth and eyes. "Is something wrong, Mr. Shaw?" She scanned the crowd nearby, hoping to see someone she knew who might stop by and rescue her. For once, there was no one.

"I saw you and my son arrived together. I hope you realize how talented a ball player he is." He tipped his head toward the field. "Heath deserves more than anything Clearwater can give him. When he heads back to Cleveland on Monday, he needs to leave with a clear conscience and put everything about this town behind him."

Raven stared at him, no longer comprehending anything he said. Heath was going back on Monday? Since when? That was less than two days away! She tried to process the news. Surely Mr. Shaw was trying to scare her. Heath would've told her himself, wouldn't he? "I'm sure if he was leaving, he'd have…" The words died on her lips as she focused on Mr. Shaw to find, for the first time, that he was smiling.

"He didn't tell you." It wasn't a question, but rather a statement with a hint of satisfaction attached to it. "I know Heath's enjoyed getting caught up with you while he's been here, but he has a big future ahead of him. He can't afford to have anyone holding him back. He was probably planning on leaving Monday and avoiding any unnecessarily messy goodbyes."

Raven's breath caught, and a pain settled over her chest. *No.* "I'm sure he was planning on telling me. Things have been so busy today, he hasn't had the chance." Not true. He had plenty of opportunities to tell her something this important.

"Maybe that's true. Well, if you see my son before I do, let him know I was looking for him. Enjoy the rest of the game."

She watched, her hands numb, as he turned and disappeared into the crowd. The sun had warmed her earlier, but now she felt chilled to the bone.

She didn't want to believe Heath would leave on Monday without saying a word. Not after this last week. After today. Did what they have stand a chance compared to the years he'd dedicated to his career?

This had to be more than just a distraction to help pass the time.

The concession stand forgotten, Raven wrapped her arms around her middle and, as if in a trance, somehow made it back to her seat.

Chapter Seventeen

Heath took in the large crowd as they watched the final play of the homecoming game. The Homecoming King and Queen were announced at halftime. As if that weren't enough for the crowd to cheer about, the Raptors were about to win the game.

He watched in satisfaction as Carl congratulated the team on a job well done. The boys' faces lit up with pride as they pounded each other on the back. There was nothing like the thrill of a win.

Heath looked to the stands, though there was no way he could see Raven through all these people. He waited long enough to congratulate each member of the Raptors, shake Carl's hand, and then he took off to find her. When Heath got to her seat, it was empty.

After scanning the crowd and seeing no signs of Raven, he pulled his phone out to find he'd received a text from her a half hour ago. He tapped on it.

"Rosie headed home early. I caught a ride home with her,

so I could change. I'll see you later at the dance."

Heath fought a wave of disappointment. He'd be taking her home himself otherwise, so it's not like their plans had changed all that much. But considering he had to go back to Cleveland on Monday, every minute with Raven counted.

People thanking him or asking for his autograph hindered Heath's trip back to his truck. Fans congratulated him and the team, as though his presence had had an impact on their win. He breathed a sigh of relief when he slid into the seat behind the wheel. Hints of lavender still lingered in the cabin as he drove home and changed.

He'd texted Raven once, asking if Rosie was feeling okay, but didn't hear back. By the time he arrived at the dance, he was getting worried about her. Afraid he'd miss her when she arrived, he stayed near the entrance. That's where Carl found him.

"Hey, Heath. Glad to see you here. I know I asked if you could help with the chaperoning tonight. Well, Rosie called me, and she may be in labor. I've got to head home. Can you do me a favor and hang out here tonight and keep an eye on the guys? Seriously, there are enough people here, so it's not a big deal. But if anyone asks, let them know where I went. Prayers are appreciated."

The poor guy checked his phone twice while he was explaining the situation. "You got it, man." Heath reached out and shook Carl's hand. "I'll be praying. Congratulations."

"Thanks!" Carl grinned before jogging to the parking lot.

Well, that was likely why he hadn't heard from Raven. He was about to head inside with the assumption that Raven had gone to the hospital as well when he saw her crossing the street. The airy purple dress she wore flowed past her knees, the fabric wrapping around her perfectly. She spotted him and waved.

"Hey, I was wondering if you were going to make it." He took her hand in his and placed a kiss to her cheek. "I just saw Carl. He's headed to the hospital."

Raven nodded. "I would go, but with Mom and Dad hovering and Carl on his way, Rosie told me to stick to my plans for tonight. I know with Mandy, it took nearly a full twenty-four hours of labor before Barry finally made his appearance."

Heath flinched at the thought of watching someone he loved go through pain for hours on end. Without warning, he pictured Raven holding their child in her arms as she brushed wisps of black hair out of the baby's face. Whoa, where had that come from? Even before, when they were engaged, he'd never pictured them having kids. Sure, it was something for the distant future. At the time, they talked about going to classes together and getting a couple years of college under their belt before getting married. This was different.

With Raven's hand tucked in his arm, he escorted her inside and observed the '80's décor. In fact, it was like stepping right into a school scene straight from *Back to the Future*. He chuckled. Fitting seeing as how he was here with the girl he'd gone to his own homecoming with. Talk about déjà vu.

There were several teachers and faculty members wandering around. Carl was right, they were set for chaperones. Good. He could focus more of his attention on the beautiful woman at his side who smelled as amazing as she looked.

They made their way around the edge of the room to the refreshment table. "Would you like some punch?"

Raven nodded, and he handed her a cup. He got one for himself and took a drink. He couldn't identify the unique combination of ingredients. "I think there may be pineapple in there. Maybe some Sprite." He took another sip, deciding that it wasn't bad, but he wouldn't get a second cup.

They watched the crowds of people laughing, talking, and dancing out on the floor. Several teens clowned around with dance moves no one had seen in years. Heath chuckled and glanced at Raven. She hadn't touched her drink.

"Not a fan of the punch?" She shook her head. Heath collected her cup and deposited it, along with his own, in the trash. When he returned, he put an arm around her and leaned close. "Would you like to dance?"

"Sure." She took his offered hand and held tight as they weaved through people to the middle of the dance floor.

The music changed to something slower, and Heath welcomed the excuse to hold her close. "I'm glad you came. If you need to go early to check on Rosie, I'll understand."

She only shook her head and put both arms around the back of his neck, resting her cheek against his shoulder. They danced like that for the duration of the song. When it ended, he reluctantly stepped back so he could see her face. The tears of sadness in her eyes weren't what he expected. "Raven? What's wrong?"

She nibbled on her bottom lip as though she were trying to decide whether to speak. The music started again, and they moved with it, but Heath sensed something was wrong, and it had nothing to do with Rosie. "Talk to me, Raven."

Just when he thought she wasn't going to respond, she raised her chin, those watery brown eyes locking on his. "Why didn't you say you were going back to Cleveland on Monday?" There was no missing the hurt in her voice. "Were you even going to tell me?"

How'd she find out? The only local people he'd told were his parents... Suddenly, Heath knew exactly what happened. He resisted the urge to clench his fist. "I found out late yesterday afternoon. I wanted us to have today—to enjoy it together—before everything else came crashing in."

Raven had her arm around his, her hand on his

shoulder. She let her forehead rest against his chest for a moment before she straightened. "So what your father said was true. You're leaving."

"I have to, Raven. Coach wants me there Monday, so I don't have a choice. Sweetheart, it's complicated." He used a finger to sweep hair away from her face and deposited it behind her ear. Oh, he hated that look of defeat in her eyes. This wasn't the place to talk; he could hardly hear himself think in here. "Come on." He held her hand and led her through the crowd and back outside. The cool breeze hit them as they exited the building, and it whipped the fabric of her skirt about her legs. How could he make Raven understand how much she meant to him? How hard it would be to leave her again?

"I should've known better." Raven shook her head as she massaged her forehead with one hand. She withdrew her other from his.

"What are you talking about?"

"This. Us. Here we are again, the burning plane crash that is Heath and Raven, take two."

"No." Heath put his hands on her shoulders. "This is different. We're different. We're going to figure out a way to make this work."

"How?" The word was barely above a whisper. "You're going to Cleveland indefinitely, and I'm here. I don't see any middle ground." She swallowed hard and sniffed. The tears in her eyes remained, as though she were keeping herself from crying by sheer will alone.

Heath's heart twisted painfully in his chest. He wanted to promise her the world. Promise her that he'd be back soon. But the truth was, he didn't know what the future held right now.

Raven's phone rang, and she took it out of the small bag she held and swiped to answer it. "Hey, Mom. Is everything—oh, no! Yes, I'll get there as soon as I can." She hung up and tossed the phone back in her bag. "Rosie's at the hospital. Her water broke and the baby's in distress. They're taking her in for an emergency C-section." She raked the fingers of both hands through her hair before she stilled and looked at Heath. "I need to go."

"I'll let someone know and come with you."

"No." The finality in her voice meant more than the word itself. "You belong here, Heath. You should stay." She turned and raced across the street, back to the parking lot.

Heath wanted to jog after her and insist on going along. Except he knew better. She needed space, and if he crowded her now, it wouldn't help his case. So he watched her walk away, feeling more helpless than he had in a long, long time.

"Honey, sit down. Your pacing is stressing me out."

Raven hardly registered Mom's words as she walked back to the window in the waiting room. It was dark outside, and all she could see were a few streetlights and the white and red lights of cars as they picked their way through the parking lot. Clouds had rolled in again, blocking her view of the stars or moon.

She turned and collapsed in the chair next to Mom with a glance at the clock on the wall. It'd been nearly an hour since she'd arrived at the hospital. Weren't emergency C-sections supposed to be fast? What if this was a bad sign? A ball of nerves shifted in the pit of her stomach. *Please, God. Guide the hands of the doctors. Protect Rosie and the baby.*

Dad reached over and patted Raven's knee. "You sure look pretty tonight. Sorry you didn't get to stay for the dance."

"It's okay, Dad. This is more important." She replayed the conversation with Heath in her mind for a tenth time, looking for any sign he might have wanted to stay in Clearwater. But as always, she kept coming up empty. It didn't matter how they felt about each other. He was leaving. The kicker? She'd known he would all along. That's what made this whole thing so ridiculous. This time, she had no one to blame but herself.

"Is everything okay?" Mom's question came at the same time Carl entered the waiting room. Everyone jumped to their feet expectantly.

Carl wore a pair of blue scrubs that included slippers over his shoes. "Tilly's fine. The cord had a knot in it and was wrapped around her neck twice. Once they delivered her and cut the cord, her vitals stabilized."

"Oh, praise God." Mom put a hand to her chest. "Is Rosie okay?"

"They're closing her up now. The surgery was more complicated than they expected, so there wasn't time to give her a spinal and they went with general anesthesia. She'll hate that she missed Tilly's birth."

Raven shook her head. "She may wish she'd been able to witness it, but she'll be so relieved to know Tilly's okay, that's all that'll matter. Wow, I'm so glad you guys got to the hospital as fast as you did."

"Me, too. I can't even..." Carl shivered. "I need to get back. Rosie made me promise to stay with Tilly as much as possible, but I knew you were all waiting and worried. I'll try to keep you updated, but they said it may be another hour or two before Rosie's in recovery."

Dad shook Carl's hand. "Congratulations, son. Go take care of my grandbaby and don't worry about us."

Carl grinned for the first time, as though the fact he was finally a father broke through the rush and worry of the night. "Thanks! I'll be back when I can." He waved and disappeared through the double doors on the other side of the room.

Mom looked at Dad, a hand over her mouth. "We have a granddaughter, Roy. Can you believe it?"

Raven smiled as the two of them embraced, joy on their faces. She couldn't wait to meet her new niece and see for herself that Rosie was okay. Carl was right.

Rosie liked to be in control and had a whole birth plan typed up for Tilly's arrival. This emergency C-section wasn't even on the contingency list. Raven could imagine the ranting Rosie would do—but only after she oohed and aahed over her new baby girl.

Her phone pinged with a message from Heath. She swiped at the screen.

"I'm praying for Rosie and the baby. Let me know how they're doing, okay?"

That he was worried about her sister and niece pulled at Raven's heartstrings. She typed out a response.

"We heard from Carl. Tilly's okay, though it was close. Rosie's in surgery. She should be fine, but it will be a while before we know more."

She silenced the phone and tossed it into her bag, hoping to hide it, along with her storm of feelings about Heath, for the time being.

Chapter Eighteen

As soon as the homecoming dance was over and guests began to clear out, Heath excused himself and headed for his truck. It'd been two hours since he'd received the text from Raven letting him know the baby was okay. He'd texted back but wasn't surprised that his phone's notifications remained empty. Whether it was poor hospital reception, that Raven was finally getting to see her sister and new niece, or that she was avoiding him, there were many reasons for her to not keep in touch.

He considered going home and waiting until tomorrow to talk to her. But as he pulled out of the school parking lot, he had another idea. Thirty minutes later, his arms full of a drink carrier and a fifth coffee in his free hand, Heath rode the elevator to the third floor of the hospital. Directions from the front desk led him to the maternity ward waiting room where he spotted Raven and her parents.

Raven was sitting in a chair, still wearing the dress she'd had on at the dance, her head resting in the crook of her arm against the back. She sat up straight when she saw him, fatigue evident in her face. Her parents noticed him then, and Mr. Weber stood and met him halfway across the room.

"Heath. It's real nice of you to come."

Heath held up the carrier. "I thought you could all use a little coffee." He lifted the extra one in his hand. "I brought one for Carl, just in case." He handed one cup to Mr. Weber and another to Mrs. Weber. "Any news about Rosie or the baby?"

Heath turned to Raven and gave her a smile along with a cup of coffee. She nodded her thanks.

"Carl hasn't been back out yet," Mrs. Weber responded. "I'll feel better when I hear Rosie is in recovery and doing okay."

Mr. Weber put an arm around his wife. "She's fine. We'll be seeing her before we know it." He took another drink of his coffee.

Mrs. Weber looked thoughtful as she nodded. "I feel so bad she had to have a C-section. I remember what it was like recovering from mine."

Raven stood. "As long as Rosie and the baby are healthy, that's the most important thing. She'll have us all here to help until she's back on her feet." She smoothed the skirt of her dress before picking up her coffee and cupping it with both hands. Her dark hair swished around her shoulders, a little disheveled since he saw her at the dance, but just as beautiful. She seemed to look everywhere but at him.

What he wanted to do was pull her away from her parents and talk about earlier. This wasn't the time or the place. However, given the fact he was leaving by lunch tomorrow, he couldn't shake a sense of urgency. She was right. He should've called her Friday evening and told her about it then. He needed Raven to understand that he didn't want to leave the same way he did last time. Yet, how was he supposed to explain how he felt when he wasn't sure himself?

He stayed for a while and listened as Mrs. Weber told the story of Rosie and Raven's birth. According to her, Rosie came out practically smiling while Raven arrived screaming at the top of her lungs.

Raven rolled her eyes and objected. Heath could totally see it, though, not that he'd tell her that. She'd always been the more outgoing and vocal of the twins.

Mrs. Weber was listing which of them had been walking, talking, and running first when Carl came back out.

He had a smile on his face and gratefully took the cup of cooled coffee from Heath with a handshake. "Rosie is in recovery, and Tilly's doing great. Six pounds, four ounces and eighteen inches long," he announced. "I want Rosie to spend a little time with Tilly first, but as soon as she gives the word, I'll come get you all so you can meet her."

There was no missing the pride in his voice as he spoke of his family.

Heath wondered if his own father had ever

spoken with such pride about him. Surely he had. Heath had faded memories of going fishing with his father or hiking outdoors. But it'd been a long time ago. Long enough that Heath sometimes wondered if he'd fabricated the events in his mind after years of wishing they'd do something together growing up. He pushed the thoughts away and turned his attention to Raven. She had a relieved smile on her face and looked more relaxed than she had since he first arrived. He didn't know Rosie or Carl all that well and certainly didn't want to intrude on the family's first chance to see the new baby.

"I think I'll head out. If I can, I'll stop by tomorrow to pay my respects to Rosie and the baby." He shook Carl's hand again. "Congratulations."

Everyone else thanked him for bringing in the coffees, including Raven. He hoped she'd walk out with him so they'd have a moment to talk. Instead, she gave him a wave, her eyes brimming with emotion.

He knew exactly how she felt.

Little Tilly was less than a day old, and Raven still couldn't get over how tiny the baby's perfect fingers and toes were. Oh, and the way those lips kept pursing together while she suckled the air as she slept. Seriously, Raven could go on holding her niece forever.

Rosie was propped up in her hospital bed as she munched on crackers and ate a little soup. Carl, on the other hand, had no problem putting his burger and fries away. He swallowed. "Thanks again for bringing lunch by, Raven. So much better than the hospital food."

"You're welcome. Sorry it was so late." Raven ran a finger over Tilly's tiny hand. "I'd bring dinner by, too, if it meant a chance to hold this little girl more. But Mom has that one covered." She flashed Rosie a smile. Raven and Mom had planned out meals for the next few days so they could help the new family of three as much as possible. Right now, Mom and Dad were home resting after the late night. "She said to let you know they'll be by with food around six-thirty."

"You are all awesome." Rosie took another sip of her soup and sighed. "I'll be glad to get home again. It's impossible to rest here. Though I'm glad to have the extra help with breastfeeding." Her gaze softened as she looked at her sleeping daughter. "I still can't believe she's here, and she's all ours."

Raven studied her new niece. Tiny wisps of light blonde hair peeked out from under her hat. She'd opened her eyes earlier, and they were a dark blue, but who knew what color they would be later. It would be fun watching this little one grow and change.

"Oh!" Rosie leaned toward the small table to her left and groaned. "Carl, can you give that envelope to Raven, please?"

"Yep." He gave his wife a firm look. Apparently they'd talked earlier about Rosie taking it easy.

Raven took the long envelope, her name across

the front in Heath's handwriting. Her breath caught as she stared at it, wondering what he'd written inside. He'd texted her this morning asking her to call him back. She'd gotten up late, rushed to church, then grabbed lunch and headed for the hospital. Sure, she could've called him while driving. Instead, she'd used the busy morning as an excuse to put their conversation off. Knowing he'd been by here and she'd missed him hit her with way more disappointment than she expected. "When did he come by?"

"It was around nine this morning." Rosie studied Raven as if hoping for a clue to what was going on. "He's driving down to San Antonio and then catching a flight from there."

Carl set his now-empty food container in the trash and went to the tiny couch in the room. He came back with a small onesie with the Clearwater Raptor logo on it. "He brought this by. I can't wait for Tilly to wear it."

What a thoughtful gift. Heath could've given Tilly something from his own team, but instead, he chose something that meant more to her family. Curiosity burned as she wondered what was in the envelope.

Little Tilly wiggled and let out a squeak. Good grief, even that was adorable. Her eyelids lifted, and she blinked up at Raven.

"Hi there, pumpkin. It's your auntie. You've got the prettiest eyes." Raven crooned at the baby for several more minutes, not caring at all if she sounded silly. Tilly listened for a bit until the need for milk overrode everything else. A desperate cry ensued, and Raven stood to hand the baby to her mama—the only one with the means to grant that request.

Rosie tried to get the baby situated. "You should go read that letter, Raven. I'm not sure what time his flight is." She gave her sister a knowing look.

Raven blinked at the envelope in her hands until Tilly's cries brought her attention back to the others in the room. "I'll give you guys some privacy. I'll be back in a while." She forced what she hoped was a normal smile before leaving.

She found a seat in the waiting room near the large wall of windows. The envelope felt heavy in her hands as she untucked the flap and withdrew a piece of paper with Heath's handwriting on it. With a deep breath, she began to read.

Raven,

I can't tell you how badly I wanted to talk to you before I left. I'm not sure if we're missing each other, or if you're avoiding me. Either way, this isn't how I wanted to leave you again.

My job is in Cleveland, and your place is here. I don't know what the answer is, sweetheart, but I'm not ready to give up on us yet.

I love you.

Always,
Heath

Raven read the letter twice, her eyes brimming

with tears. She blinked past them, sending several cascading down her cheeks. Heath would be in San Antonio by now. She withdrew her phone, noting the missed call and text. She'd chosen to mute it before church and then forgot. Ironic considering yesterday she'd avoided him, not knowing what to say or do, and today she'd accomplished the same by accident.

With a sniff, she brushed the moisture off her cheeks and hit his number. It rang four times before voicemail kicked in. Raven listened to Heath's deep voice for a few moments before hanging up. He was probably on the plane now, unable to use his cell phone.

She was too late.

Did he think she'd dismissed his letter because she hadn't contacted him? That bothered her as much as anything else. But then, what would she have said if she had called him? That she loved him too? Raven groaned and rested her head in her hands. "What am I supposed to do, God? It'd be so much easier if You'd give me a clear sign."

She sighed. There was no divine intervention. No answer written in sparkling lights.

Heath was on a plane somewhere between Texas and Ohio, but it felt like he might as well have been on his way to the moon.

~*~

What a ridiculously long flight. It didn't help that

Heath had left his heart back in Clearwater. With each passing minute on the plane, he wondered if Raven had gotten his note and whether he'd hear from her. He wished he had more notice before going back to Cleveland. Even another week would've given him time to figure out his next move.

It was after eight in the evening when the plane landed. Heath immediately turned his phone back on. Relief flooded his system when he saw that he'd missed a call from Raven. He sent her a text.

"I just landed. Will call you back as soon as I can."

It took forever for the plane to taxi to the gate where everyone disembarked. Heath wheeled his suitcase up the ramp and into the cooler air of the airport. He decided to take a taxi to his apartment where his own car waited for him.

Once he got through the gate congestion, he found a spot near the exit and sat on a bench and dialed Raven's number. She answered on the second ring. "Hey. You get there okay?"

"I did." Hearing her voice made Heath relax more than he'd been able to all day. He leaned against the back of the bench. "It was a long flight. How are Rosie and Tilly doing?"

"They're doing well. The doctors think they'll be able to go home on Tuesday if everything continues like it has."

"That's great news." He paused and wiped a sweaty palm against his pants. "Did you get my note?"

"Yes. I'm sorry I missed your call and text earlier.

I'd silenced my phone for church and forgot to turn it back on. I never forget." She was rambling, and he could picture her cheeks getting red and her hands waving in gestures. The thought made him smile as she continued. "I didn't realize you were leaving so soon today. It was stupid… I should have called you back yesterday. I guess I needed time to think." Her voice sounded sad.

"It'll be okay, Raven. I'm going to get back to Clearwater as soon as I can. There's a lot we need to talk about, and time isn't our friend here." He wished he could see her face right now. He closed his eyes and pictured that pretty smile of hers and those eyes that always held him captive. Were they even remotely on the same page? "I'll send you my address here and let you know as soon as I do when I'll be flying back." Even as he said the words, he knew his coach wouldn't be thrilled with him leaving any time soon. "We'll figure this out." There was silence on the other end. "Raven?"

"I'm still here." Another stretch of silence. "We tried this once, Heath, and it didn't work. What makes us think this will be any different?"

"Because I refuse to give up on us this time."

Chapter Nineteen

Raven flopped onto Mandy's couch and reached for the laundry basket on the floor by her feet. It was filled with a sea of blue, white, and green little boy clothes. She folded a cute shirt with a shark on it and put it on the coffee table.

"You don't have to do that." Mandy tossed her an amused look. "I think I can fold my own laundry."

"Well, seeing as I showed up unannounced, it's the least I can do." Raven folded a pair of socks together, marveling at how tiny they were. Yet these clothes looked large compared to Tilly's newborn things. She watched Mandy for a minute as she stacked blocks and then waited for Barry to knock them down.

As soon as he did, Barry erupted in giggles. He was sitting in front of the pile of blocks, clapping his hands, as he waited for Mandy to create another tower. "This is one of our favorite games." She reached out and lovingly brushed hair out of her son's eyes. "But trust me, if you want to grace me with adult conversation *and* fold my laundry, I'm not going to tell you no." She watched Raven for a moment. "So what brings you to my neck of the woods on a Thursday afternoon?"

"I called into work sick. Needing a mental health day counts, right?"

"Seeing as I could count on a finger the number of times you've taken one, I'd definitely agree with that. Does the catalyst for such a monumental occasion happen to be playing football in Ohio?"

Raven flinched. "Maybe." She folded a few more articles of clothing before leaning into the corner of the couch. "Heath and I talk on the phone every evening, but it's not the same. There's a lot we're not saying, and I feel like the pressure's building, waiting to explode." She shrugged. "My parents think I should go to Ohio. After he left the first time, I feel like he should be the one to make the grand gesture. Is that silly?"

"What kind of gesture are you wanting?"

Raven's face warmed. "I guess I spent months after he left the first time hoping he'd decide he couldn't live without me and that being together was worth more than anything else." She made a face. "Yeah, that sounds dumb now."

"Not dumb, Raven. Just not realistic now. Playing football is Heath's job. He's probably got a contract with the team. How long has he lived in Cleveland? He has an apartment there. A life." When

Raven's face fell, Mandy held up a hand. "I'm not saying he doesn't want you two to be together, or that he's not considering your relationship a priority. But let's face it. Choices were made, lives were lived, and that doesn't go away like this." Mandy snapped her fingers.

Barry studied his own hand, opening and closing it as though he were trying to mimic his mom. Both women smiled at his antics.

Raven gave up on folding clothes. Instead, she sank to the floor with her back against the couch and welcomed a cuddle from her favorite baby boy. "Part of me wants to throw everything to the wind and go to Cleveland. But Rosie just had the baby, and I had enough of my parents trying to push me to go after Heath that first year he left. Not to mention you, and Chrissy, and my job. I can't leave it all behind. Besides, what if he's decided the life he built there is better than anything we could have together?"

"I seriously doubt that's the case." Mandy looked thoughtful. "Okay, how about this? Take all of those complications out of the equation. If it was only you and Heath, what would you do?"

Raven thought for several heartbeats. "I'd go to Cleveland. But it's not that easy. My job—"

"What you do is in high demand, Raven. You could find a job anywhere as a physical therapy assistant." She crossed her arms. "And we've talked about how the pay at CRC is way below the national average for what you do. You could probably get a better-paying job up there." She raised an eyebrow in challenge. "What other excuses do you have?"

There was a whole string of reasons why these weren't excuses, but the more Raven thought about it, the sillier they became. "My parents have been on my case about Heath all week. If I go, they'll never let me live it down."

Mandy laughed at that one. "So they've been wrong about a lot of stuff most of your life. They were bound to get something right eventually. Don't let that stop you from finding love and happiness and all that. Give them a check mark in the win column and move on."

"Hey, I thought I was the painfully blunt side of this friendship." Raven tried to force a serious glare, but it was clear from Mandy's amused smile it wasn't convincing.

"Sometimes the tables need to be turned, my friend." She picked Barry up and patted his back for a few moments before the little guy was on the move again. He inched his way forward on his belly to reach a toy that went straight into his mouth. "Now, where were we? Oh, that's right. We took care of your job and your parents. As for Rosie and her family, me, and Chrissy, I think we'll survive. We've got social media and phone calls. Unless you're planning on being a recluse, you're bound to get down here for a visit now and again. And I've always wanted to go on a vacation to Lake Erie."

The possibility of leaving Clearwater and

everyone in it brought tears to Raven's eyes. But at the same time, she could hear a conversation she had with Heath a few weeks ago echo in her mind. *"You could've come home any time, Heath."* Wasn't that the same for her as well? Just because she left didn't mean she was never coming back again.

The thought fueled the speck of hope in her heart, and a slow smile transformed her face. "I guess I'm going to Cleveland." She got to her feet and walked to the big picture window and back again. "I need to reserve a plane ticket. Oh, and convince Fay to give me tomorrow off, too. Can I book a flight on such short notice?" She stopped her pacing. "What do I say to Heath?"

Mandy stood then, a big grin on her face. "I think you know the answer to that. As for the rest, why don't you call Fay, and I'll bring up some websites so we can go shopping for a ticket?"

"Yeah. Okay." Raven's hands shook as she took her phone out. She walked back to the picture window again and found the CRC phone number in her list of contacts. As the phone rang, she smiled at the image of herself reflected in the glass pane. A grand gesture was exactly what they needed, and no one said it was Heath who had to make it.

~*~

Heath walked out of the fancy office building and into the chilly air Friday afternoon. He was happier than he'd been in a long time. No, not happy. Free. He spun his keyring around a finger as he trekked across the parking lot to his car. There was a lot of work to do to put his plan into motion, but today he'd taken the first major step.

He sang out loud to whatever song came on the radio and drove across town to his little apartment. After parking in his usual spot, he took the stairs two at a time, coming to a halt when he saw Raven sitting on the step in front of his door. She jumped to her feet the moment she heard him approach.

"Hi, Heath." She looked uncertain as she shuffled her feet. Her cheeks and nose were red thanks to the chilly air.

Heath looked up at the clouds building with rain in the forecast. "How long have you been waiting here? You've got to be freezing." He moved forward then stopped. "Is everything okay?" Her nervous expression was making him anxious as well.

Raven shrugged. "I wanted to surprise you. Then I took a taxi here and realized maybe I didn't think things through." She laughed. "The longer I waited, the more I wondered whether I should've called first. Maybe you'd rather I didn't—"

He wasn't about to let her finish that statement. He covered the distance between them in three long strides and enveloped her in his arms. The contented sigh she released as he covered her lips with his own confirmed everything he'd set in motion today. He kissed one of her cheeks, the chill of her skin reminding him that she needed to get inside. "Here, let me open the door…"

Raven shook her head. "Wait. There's something I need to say. If I don't say it now…"

Well, that guaranteed his undivided attention. He studied her face as she took a step backward. "We can talk inside."

She ignored him and took a deep breath. "Look, I know this is presumptuous, but I spent most of last night browsing different employment sites. I think I could get a job here as a physical therapist assistant pretty easily. I haven't talked to Fay about it yet, but I'm certain she'd give me a letter of recommendation."

Heath blinked at her, trying to process the words she was throwing at him. "Wait. What are you talking about?"

Raven ran her hands through her hair, gathering it all together and twisting it at the base of her neck. "This long-distance stuff isn't working, Heath. And I refuse to spend the next years of my life wondering what would've happened if…" Her voice caught. "I can relocate here. It might take a couple of weeks to get everything figured out." She stopped, her eyes searching his. "If that's what you want, too."

He reached for her hand. "What about your family and Clearwater? That's your home."

"I can always go back and visit. But my home is with you."

Heath's heart expanded and tripped over itself as he absorbed the sincerity in her eyes. "You are my home, too, sweetheart." He tugged on her hand, bringing her back into his arms where he kissed her until they were both breathless. He rested a hand on each of her cheeks and smiled. "Now will you come inside where it's warmer?"

She nodded. He unlocked the door and led her inside. Raven stopped, taking in the room full of boxes. "Did you just move in? I was thinking you'd had this apartment for a while."

Heath put an arm around her shoulders and placed a kiss to her temple. "No. I'm moving out."

"What? I don't understand."

"I got back from signing the paperwork. I took early retirement, Raven, so I could come back to you in Clearwater."

Raven's jaw dropped. She turned to look at him, her eyes filled with tears. "Are you serious?"

Heath laughed. "Yes, sweetheart, I'm dead serious." He brushed some hair off her forehead. "I spoke with the team's physical therapist here, and after working on the field, we agreed that I would never be back to my full strength again. I've felt that would be the case for a long while, but I needed the doctor to confirm. Besides, I guess my heart wasn't in playing football anymore. Not when it meant I have to be away from you."

"But what will you do in Clearwater?"

"I own several businesses in town. I'm sure I can find something to keep myself busy." He winked. "Wait here for a minute." He retrieved a small box from his side table and slipped it into a pocket before returning. "This isn't exactly how I planned it, but I can't think of better timing." With that, he withdrew the box and opened it, revealing the engagement ring he'd put on her finger once before.

Heath took her left hand in his. "My sweet Raven. I promise I will not leave your side until my last breath. All I want is to spend the rest of our lives showing you how much I love you." He watched as Raven covered her mouth with her free hand and a tear escaped the corner of her eye. "Will you marry me?"

"Yes."

Her breathless answer was all he needed. Heath slid the ring on her finger, happy to see it still fit. She stepped into his embrace, fitting perfectly into his arms.

"I love you, Heath."

"I love you, too."

Chapter Twenty
December 31st

Raven buried her nose in a lavender bouquet and breathed in deep. She only lifted her head when Rosie laughed.

"You aren't getting cold feet, are you?" She shifted two-month-old Tilly to her shoulder.

"No." She shot her sister a look of warning which was promptly ignored. "But I am worried about tripping over my shoes, running over the flower girl, or something else just as mortifying." When she'd chosen fresh lavender for her wedding bouquet, she'd had no idea how much she'd need its calming effects.

"You have nothing to worry about," Mandy assured her as she buzzed around Raven's head with a can of hairspray and a brush. "You look gorgeous, and even if you do trip and fall, I'm sure Heath won't mind catching you and carrying you to the altar." She winked.

"That's not even funny." Raven giggled anyway, thankful for friends who always found a way to make her laugh. She glanced at Chrissy with a smile. "I wish I could drink coffee right now to calm my nerves."

"And risk spilling it on that dress? Not a chance."

Raven turned to look at herself in the mirror. She'd thought the dress was perfect the moment she saw it in the store. It looked even better now. Embroidered flowers covered the cream-colored fabric. It gave the whole dress a pretty, detailed look. The fabric hugged her waist and hips before flaring out into a beautiful floor-length skirt and a train that was just the right length.

No, she didn't want to spill coffee on this dress. She couldn't wait for Heath to see her wearing it.

The thought had her pulse racing again. "How much longer?"

"Fifteen minutes." Rosie's, Mandy's, and Chrissy's voices combined in a chorus that had everyone laughing. They gathered around Raven until they could see each other in the mirror.

Raven looked at each of them, thankful Rosie could be her maid of honor, and her two best friends her bridesmaids. "You ladies rock. Seriously, thank you for everything."

The door opened and Mom came through. The moment she saw Raven, she fanned her face to keep the tears at bay. "Oh, honey. Look at you. Beautiful. I'm so happy both of my daughters will finally be married. Think about it: your babies can grow up together. Oh, it'll be so much fun to see the cousins playing!"

Raven rolled her eyes at Rosie before placing a hand on each of their mother's shoulders. "Let's get me married first, huh? I'm pretty sure popping out babies while walking down the aisle is frowned upon."

Mom gave her an exasperated look. "I wanted you to know your father's waiting downstairs. We'll be starting the ceremony soon." She gathered Raven's hands in her own. "I'm so happy." She kissed Raven's cheek before leaving.

Rosie patted Tilly's diapered bottom. "I'll go hand this baby girl off to her daddy and be right back."

Raven called over her shoulder. "Will you do me a favor and see if Heath's father made it in?"

"Of course."

Raven chewed on her bottom lip for a second before Mandy smacked her arm. "Stop that, you're messing up your gloss." She grabbed the tube of lip gloss and reapplied it. "I take it Mr. Shaw still isn't speaking to Heath? That's so sad."

Raven frowned. "Ever since they had that big blow up over Heath's decision to retire, Mr. Shaw hasn't spoken to him. Heath asked him to be his best man and was going to try and convince him to come this morning. One of his groomsmen will stand in if Mr. Shaw doesn't show, but I'm hoping it won't come to that." The thought of something so hurtful marring their wedding made Raven both sad and angry for her future husband.

"That's horrible." Chrissy shook her head. "It was big of Heath to ask him to be his best man despite everything."

The door opened again, and Rosie returned with a smile on her face. "Believe it or not, Mr. Shaw is downstairs and in position. Okay, your dad is on his way, Raven. The rest of us should go."

The ladies held hands as Mandy led them in a prayer of blessing over the day and the couple's future together. There was a knock at the door as they all echoed "Amen."

Rosie, Mandy, and Chrissy slipped out before Raven's dad entered the room. He stood looking at her, tears in his eyes.

"My baby girl, you are beautiful. I can't believe my youngest daughter is finally getting married."

For once, the comment about being the youngest by two minutes didn't bother her one bit. Instead, she slipped her hand through his arm and smiled up at him. "Thanks, Daddy."

"Are you ready for this?"

She nodded.

"Good. Because I don't think I am." He squeezed her hand and led her out of the room. They maneuvered their way down the short flight of stairs to the main level of the church.

The music played, and after a time Dad escorted Raven down the aisle. She basked in the love and support of her family, friends, and community.

But it was the man who stood at the end that truly drew her forward. Those blue eyes of his watched her every step, filled with the kind of love she'd only imagined before meeting him. When Dad placed her hand in Heath's, she knew this was where she belonged.

Heath pressed a kiss to her hand and then held it firmly in his. They turned to face the pastor, and the ceremony began.

A few minutes into the ceremony, the pastor encouraged them to exchange vows. Heath smiled into her eyes. "Raven, from the moment I met you, I knew you were the one for me. We've had some hiccups along the way," there were chuckles around the room, including a teary one from Raven, "and we've spent way more time apart than I would've liked. But tomorrow is the first day of a new year. It's fitting because it's also the first day of our lives together. I praise God each day that you gave me a second chance, and I'll spend every breath He gives me loving you." He slipped the wedding ring on her finger and kissed it.

How was Raven supposed to follow that when she had a lump in her throat and was doing her best not to cry? She sniffed and blinked rapidly to clear the tears. Heath reached up and swiped her cheek with his thumb.

She cleared her throat and focused on their joined hands. "I used to think of the years we spent apart and only saw what was missing. But now I understand we needed that time to grow and change into who we are today." She raised her chin and gazed into his eyes. "You are my best friend and the man who holds the key to my heart. What we went through was hard, but I wouldn't change a thing because it brought us to where we are now. I'm proud of who *you* are. I can't wait to spend the rest of my life with you."

The softness and love in his eyes followed her movements as she slid his wedding ring onto his finger.

The pastor smiled and put a hand on each of their shoulders. "Now by the power vested in me by the City of Clearwater, it is my honor and delight to declare you husband and wife. You may kiss the bride."

Raven gave a little squeak as Heath scooped her into his arms and gave her a kiss that had her toes tingling. When they parted, everyone in the room was clapping, whooping, and whistling. Her cheeks grew warm, but she waved to the crowd as Heath held her close.

"You're not going to drop me, are you?" she teased, one of her palms resting on the side of his face.

"Are you kidding? I have no intention of ever letting you go again." His lips touched hers again in a kiss that promised forever.

Thank you!

I appreciate you for taking the time to read **Marrying Raven**. I hope you enjoyed it and will consider leaving a review on Amazon and/or Goodreads. I like hearing what you think about it, and it'll help other readers discover new books as well.

If you've liked the Brides of Clearwater books, you might enjoy the complete Love's Compass series as well.

Acknowledgments

Marrying Raven would never have come together if it weren't for the love, grace, and patience that God has seen fit to send my way. It is my prayer that He uses this book to bless others.

Many thanks to the wonderful people who took the time to read, critique, and help me edit this book: Steph, Mom (Suzanne), Rachel, Kris, Shanna, Denny, Sandy, and Heather. I appreciate you all!

This book cover is one of my favorites, and it never would have come together if it weren't for the photography talents of Jennifer from Jennifer Pitts Photography and Vicki's design skills at Blue Valley Author Services. Thank you, ladies, for this gorgeous cover that fits Raven's book so perfectly.

About the Author

Melanie D. Snitker has enjoyed writing fiction for as long as she can remember. She started out creating episodes of cartoon shows she wanted to see as a child, and her love of writing grew from there. She and her husband live in Texas with their two children, who keep their lives full of adventure, and two dogs, who add a dash of mischief to the family dynamics. In her spare time, Melanie enjoys photography, reading, crocheting, baking, and hanging out with family and friends.

http://www.melaniedsnitker.com
https://twitter.com/MelanieDSnitker
https://www.facebook.com/melaniedsnitker

Subscribe to Melanie's newsletter and receive a monthly e-mail containing recipes, information about new releases, giveaways, and more! You can find a link to sign up on her website.

Books by Melanie D. Snitker

Calming the Storm
(A Marriage of Convenience)

Love's Compass Series:
Finding Peace (Book 1)
Finding Hope (Book 2)
Finding Courage (Book 3)
Finding Faith (Book 4)
Finding Joy (Book 5)
Finding Grace (Book 6)

Life Unexpected Series:
Safe In His Arms (Book 1)
Someone to Trust (Book 2)

Welcome to Romance
Finding Forever in Romance

Brides of Clearwater Series:
Marrying Mandy (Book 1)
Marrying Raven (Book 2)